QUEENS OF CYBERSPACE

PRESS START

Clancy Teitelbaum

EPIC
Press

Press Start
Queens of Cyberspace: Book #1

Written by Clancy Teitelbaum

Copyright © 2016 by Abdo Consulting Group, Inc.

Published by EPIC Press™
PO Box 398166
Minneapolis, MN 55439

Cover design by Laura Mitchell
Images for cover art obtained from iStockPhoto.com
Edited by Jennifer Skogen

Library of Congress Cataloging-in-Publication Data

Teitelbaum, Clancy.
Press START / Clancy Teitelbaum.
p. cm. — (Queens of cyberspace; #1)
Summary: Suzanne Thurston and her two best friends, Brit and Mikayla, couldn't
be more different. What all three girls have in common is Io, the fantasy video game
that Suzanne designed. As Io's first and only players, the girls battle monsters and go
on royal quests, but things begin to go wrong in the game, and the girls find themselves stuck inside a virtual world that appears to be very real and deadly.
ISBN 978-1-68076-197-9 (hardcover)
1. Friendship—Fiction. 2. Computer games—Fiction. 3. Internet—Fiction.
4. Virtual reality—Fiction. 5. Cyberspace—Fiction. 6. Video games—Fiction.
7. Young adult fiction. I. Title.
[Fic]—dc23
2015949423

EPIC
Press

For my parents

Chapter 1

The Meadow of Beginnings was a lovely meadow, as big as a sea. You couldn't fault someone for making the comparison. The tall grasses and wildflowers waving in the breeze resembled nothing so much as an ocean of vegetation. The brilliantly blue sky was free of clouds, the breeze was pleasant, and the temperature was cool. Short trees rose up from the grass at regular intervals, their roots covered by soft mounds of earth. By each little tree sprang a little spring. The stream water was clear and refreshing and restored twenty HP per liter consumed.

The Meadow extended infinitely in every direction. You couldn't reach its end. To try and do so would not only be foolish, but would also lead to you missing the beauty all around you. And not just the beauty of the Meadow, but the beauty of many of its inhabitants as well.

Flitting from flower to flower, drinking their fill of nectar, pollen smeared on their faces, faeries of every color joked and jabbered as faeries often do. They were tiny beings, hardly bigger than butterflies. And like butterflies their wings were beautiful. Iridescent, at one second they shown a deep crimson red, then a neon green, and then an electric violet.

One can always tell how a faerie feels by its wing-color. When a faerie is content, the colors are calming: deep blues and luxuriant purples. When agitated, their wings take on more vivid hues like burning reds, neon greens, and jagged yellows.

The most beauteous of the faeries—his name was Ipsamil, but no one cared to check—alighted on the petals of a daffodil and bowed low to drink from its nectar. Another soon joined him, and they conversed in their singsong, twittering language. It sounded like two birds laughing, a magical sound filling all who heard it with a sense of wonder and awe.

Of course, the only non-faeries who could have heard weren't listening. And they weren't watching as the faeries began their elaborate courtship ritual. But then, they had other matters on their minds.

Brit, for example, had just been hit by a goblin Mage's Fire Blast. Her armor ate most of the damage but the spell's knockback sent her flying. She landed ass-first on the faeries' daffodil. Their wings turned pitch black in terror before they were squished. Instant death.

Brit didn't realize she had landed on anything. You don't get XP for killing faeries.

Grumbling, she weeded around in the tall grass, looking for her halberd. She had dropped it when the Fire Blast hit her straight in the chest. After ripping up a square foot of turf she found her halberd and charged back into battle. The other faeries fled in terror as the two smeared across the seat of Brit's armor exploded into a cloud of pixels.

By now, the cool down for Fire Blast was over.

The goblin Mage raised his staff high and began muttering a new incantation. He was the height of a child, with a snaggle-toothed sneer permanently stamped on his face. His skin was a fetid white, the color of mold. Brit could barely see him over the tall grass, but she could see the red diamond twirling above his head, marking him as an enemy.

The spell he was casting would have knocked Brit on her ass again, if he got the chance to cast it. Before he could finish, Suzanne sprang up from the tall grass behind the Mage, and with a quick slash of her long dagger, removed his pointy-eared head from his shoulders.

Instantly, the goblin began pixelating, like the faeries. But with the goblin, Brit saw the process clearly. First, his body, including the severed head, began to distort. It seemed to stretch and shrink at the same time, to grow corners and edges where none had been. The distortion only lasted a second. With a small pop, the goblin's body burst apart into pixels, which floated down to the ground, flurries of glittering snow vanishing before they landed.

You don't get XP for killing a faerie, but a goblin Mage, at Suzanne's level, gave her twenty-five. She watched the number in the bottom right-hand corner of her vision climb up to four thirty-one. At five hundred, she'd advance to level six and all her stats would jump.

Sixty-nine to go, she told herself. Then she dove to the ground, eating a mouthful of grass as she dodged a second goblin Mage's energy blast.

Where the first goblin's body had been, a small, glowing treasure chest appeared. It floated and spun in the air. Before Suzanne got to it, Brit ran by and slapped the top of the chest. A short jingle played, signifying that the items formerly in the chest had just been added to Brit's inventory.

Without breaking pace, Brit spun around, smashing the blade of her halberd into the stomach of the second Mage. Like a home run off the slugger's bat, the goblin was lifted into the air and sent hurtling away.

Grinning, Brit jogged over to help Suzanne up.

Suzanne wasn't nearly as happy. "Hey!" she shouted. "That was my kill! You stole my loot!"

"Then what's it doing in my inventory?" Brit asked.

"That's bullshit," Suzanne yelled.

Brit stuck out her tongue. "If you can't get loot, you can always make the game easier."

Suzanne flipped her off and struggled to come up with a retort. Before she could produce any material, she heard Mikayla shout, "Hey, a little help here?"

Mikayla was backed up to the nearest tree by a trio of goblin Lancers. A few paces behind the Lancers stood the leader of the bunch, an Assassin named Igor Redcap. A floating red crown over Igor's head marked him as the area boss for the Meadow of Beginnings.

One of the Lancers advanced, thrusting a barbed spear at Mikayla's knees. She stomped on the spearhead, snapping it off the shaft. A quick cuff with the shield strapped to her left arm sent the goblin tumbling back, head over heels, into the grass. It stayed on the ground, deciding that playing dead would keep it alive longer.

The second Lancer saw this as his chance and tried

to stab Mikayla in the back. Suzanne saw the goblin make its move and she pulled a throwing knife from her belt. From this range she had a seventy-three percent chance of hitting it. The blade whizzed through the air, planting itself in the Lancer's back. The goblin fell to the ground and didn't get back up.

Mikayla flashed her a thumbs-up before immediately swinging her arm to parry a spear-thrust with her shield. The goblin drew back its spear to try again, but by then Brit had reached the melee. She punted the goblin away into the Meadow.

The remaining two Lancers began to struggle to their feet. Mikayla had all the time in the world to draw her estoc, a thin sword for stabbing and slashing. With two quick thrusts, she transformed the goblins into a cloud of pixels.

Brit and Mikayla high-fived. The other low-level goblins stayed long enough to watch their comrades pixelate before they ran off into the Meadow.

Which left only Igor Redcap.

He was twice the size of the other goblins. He drew

his scimitar, its blade stained red with what looked like blood.

"Alright," he growled. "I'll do it meself."

He swung the curved sword around in an impressive display of swordsmanship. It hummed as it cut through the air, whirring faster and faster until it was too fast to follow with the human eye. Fortunately, Mikayla's vision was buffed up.

"Well, shit," Brit said. "This must be the boss, huh?"

Mikayla nodded. They took a step back as the murderous Redcap advanced.

"Come on then," he growled. "Let's have some fun."

A devilish grin spread across the goblin's face. A second later it was replaced with a look of shock. His eyes rolled upwards, staring at the throwing knife that seemed to sprout from between his eyebrows.

Mikayla and Brit turned to see Suzanne, her arm still extended in the follow-through of her throw. Redcap sputtered once and lurched forward, before keeling over and joining his comrades in pixelation.

"I swear, if either of you steal this loot I'm throwing the next knife at you."

Suzanne jogged over to the floating chest that appeared where Redcap had fallen and placed a hand on it. As the jingle played, Suzanne saw her experience points increase to four eighty-one. She was almost at the next level.

Suddenly, 7:00 A.M. appeared in the sky in large, blinking, black numbers. They were nothing like the numbers in the girls' personal displays. Those showed experience points in the lower right-hand corner of their screen and health and Energite bars in the upper left. The blinking numbers indicated the alarm that Suzanne had set to make sure they wouldn't be late for school.

"Guess it's time to log out," Mikayla said, half sighing. She waved her hand in front of her, opening her Player Menu. She scrolled through the list of options, represented to her as floating blue boxes, until she came to the last one, marked END SESSION.

She selected it and instantly vanished.

Brit did the same. Suzanne waited for a second,

looking around the Meadow. They'd stayed up all night playing, but she didn't feel tired in the least. And in game time, one night had stretched into what felt like a few days.

The breeze picked up. Off in the distance, Suzanne could see the faeries returning to their flowers, resuming their irreverent routine. She shouted a greeting at the little beings. Afraid of more squishing, the faeries flew for cover.

But by then Suzanne had vanished back into reality.

Chapter 2

Suzanne disengaged from the TII. All she could see was sucked away from her until it formed a single pixel in the center of her field of vision. Then the pixel flickered out.

She reached out with her arms—her real arms—and fumbled with the helmet. Her fingers were like rubber, so first she had to work the feeling back into them. After some flexing, she was able to lift the TII off her head. The electrodes which lined the insides of the helmet made popping noises as they broke off. She blinked, letting her eyes adjust back to reality, and taking in her surroundings.

In her hands was the TII. It looked like a motorcycle

helmet sans visor. A long cord trailed from the back of the neck to a computer humming on Suzanne's remarkably untidy desk. The desk was a hand-me-down monster. It filled one corner of the room, loose bits of paper competing for desktop space with three gargantuan monitors. A digital picture frame, showing a slideshow of a younger Suzanne with her parents, was crammed in alongside empty mechanical pencils and old notebooks for school.

Instead of standing in the Meadow of Beginnings, in the virtual world of Io, Suzanne was sitting on her bed, propped up against the headboard with some pillows. The walls of her room were covered with posters. SUDA51 and teenage Bill Gates hung opposite enlarged stills from *Fullmetal Alchemist, Sword Art Online*, and *One Piece*. Over her bed was a Zerg banner from *Starcraft II*. Interspersed among the posters were smaller pictures of her hanging out with Brit and Mikayla.

The light of early morning crept through the window behind her desk. Suzanne pulled her straight black hair back into a loose ponytail and lazily checked the monitors. The computer was saving their latest gaming session.

Then she saw the digital clock display on her desktop. It was already seven fifteen. They had half an hour to get to homeroom.

"Shit," Suzanne muttered. She stood up, still unsteady on her real legs. She was always a little off-balance after returning from the digital world. It didn't help that she'd spent last night gaming instead of sleeping.

Mikayla already had her helmet off and was rubbing her eyes with her hands, trying to help them readjust. There were circles beneath her eyes.

Brit, slumped into a beanbag chair, still had her TII helmet on.

"Two more minutes," she said drowsily, when Suzanne knocked on her helmet.

Mikayla looked down at her day-old clothes and sighed. She walked over to Brit and kicked her in the leg.

"Come on, lazy ass. We're already late."

Ten minutes later they had changed their clothes,

washed their faces, and repacked their bags. Brit and Mikayla were already out the door into the hallway of the apartment building when Suzanne heard her father call from the kitchen.

"Honey, can you come in here?"

Mikayla gave Suzanne an exasperated look. They didn't have time for this.

"It'll just take a second," Suzanne said. She called back into the apartment, "Coming!"

Her dad was sitting at the kitchen table. The day's news was open on his tablet, but it was clear that he hadn't even glanced it over. He was wearing his usual bathrobe and pajama pants. It had been a few days since his last shave.

When Suzanne looked at pictures of herself and her father, she saw that their most similar feature was their nose. For everything else, she looked more like her mom. She wondered if that was what her dad was seeing as he glanced her over. She was nearly as unkempt as he was.

He didn't say anything at first, just swirled around

the contents of his mug. The microwave's clock said it was already seven twenty-eight.

"Dad, I've got to go."

He nodded, taking a sip from his mug. "Just," he said, searching for the right words. "Just have a good day, and be safe, okay?"

Suzanne nodded, trying to not show how tired she was. She wasn't supposed to be staying up all night playing games, but her dad never noticed. After four years, he was still getting used to being a single parent.

He smiled and stood up to hug her. Holding her tight, he said, "I love you more than anything in this world or any other. You know that, right?"

Suzanne knew. She just didn't want to talk about it when she was going to be late for school. Outside, Mikayla honked on the horn.

"I've got to go," she repeated.

He let her go and smiled.

"Knock 'em dead," he said.

She ran to catch up with the other girls. Brit had her window down and was making a big deal about leaving Suzanne behind. Mikayla had both hands on the wheel and roared off as soon as Suzanne climbed into the backseat.

"What were you doing—eating breakfast?" Brit joked.

"Shut up and look for cops," Mikayla said. She was using her I'm-a-captain-don't-fuck-with-me voice. "We're going to break a lot of laws."

Mikayla was one of the captains of the cheer squad—a feat made more remarkable by the fact that she was still just a junior. She was wearing her uniform right now, crimson and white. Most of the cheerleaders wore their hair up in pigtails but Mikayla kept her hair in a short afro.

Suzanne thought cheer squad was an oxymoron considering how miserable it made Mikayla most of the time.

"I can't get a tardy because then I'll get detention," Mikayla said, swerving across three lanes. She cut another car off at a stop sign. "I can't get detention because then I'll miss practice."

Suzanne had heard this all before. She wished Mikayla

would pay more attention to the other cars on the road but was too busy holding on to say anything.

"What's it matter if you miss practice?" Brit asked. "You're the best at it, right? It's not like they'd take the field without you."

Mikayla sighed. "That's exactly what it's like."

Suzanne, like Brit, didn't get why Mikayla would waste every afternoon practicing getting thrown in the air and making human pyramids, but Suzanne never really understood sports in general. She'd always been what guidance counselors called an "indoors kid."

"Anyway," Mikayla said, accelerating through a yellow light, "I have to stay on the team. If I get kicked off, there goes my excuse for gaming all night with you knuckleheads."

"It was a great Spirit Sleepover," Brit laughed.

Spirit Sleepovers were an ingenious invention of Mikayla's. As far as her parents knew they were bonding rituals before pep rallies. In truth, they were an excuse she gave her parents whenever she was going over to Suzanne's to game all night. So far, the bluff had worked, but Suzanne always felt uneasy when Brit and

Mikayla talked about lying to their parents. Of course, Suzanne never really had to lie to hers. Thinking about that made her uneasy too.

Miraculously, they arrived at Perry Hall High School without driving any other cars off the road. Right as they reached the doors, the bell rang.

Mikayla groaned. "Great. Absolutely perfect."

Brit rolled her eyes. "I'll handle it," she said. "Like I always do."

"You're the best," Mikayla trilled, holding the door open for Suzanne to enter.

When they reached their homeroom, Brit went in first. A minute later their homeroom teacher, Mr. Wells, came tearing out of the room, his car keys in his hand and a worried expression on his face. Brit stuck her head out the door and motioned them into the room. Mikayla and Suzanne had to cover their mouths to stifle their giggles.

"What did you tell him?" Suzanne asked.

"I said I saw his car getting towed. The hitch pulled his bumper off."

The other students were engaged in their own

conversations or copying homework for other classes. A few looked up and waved to Mikayla, who smiled and waved back. Sometimes being friends with Mikayla made Suzanne feel completely invisible.

Brit walked over to Mr. Wells's desk, where homeroom attendance was pulled up on his computer. She changed Suzanne and Mikayla's record to reflect they were on time before going back and editing out of some of her own past offenses. Satisfied, she joined the other girls at their usual table.

Soon after, Mr. Wells returned to the classroom.

"It wasn't my car," he panted, hands on his knees.

Mr. Wells's heart was clearly not in teaching. He taught Intro to Technology, a notoriously easy class. Most days he lectured from the slideshows the county provided, although every so often he broke the monotony by showing an educational film. The movies were instructional how-to's, relics from the eighties that featured such cutting-edge technology as floppy disks and dial-up modems.

But the students liked Mr. Wells because he was young enough to laugh at their jokes and because he wanted to be in school as little as they did. Suzanne wondered how he'd ended up in the job, but she didn't think about it too hard. Intro to Tech was the one class she looked forward to every day. It was the one class where she got forty-five minutes and a computer to do whatever she wanted.

Sure, there was coursework, but Mr. Wells was as inattentive with grades as he was with everything else. The only thing he was a stickler for was attendance, mostly because that was a school-wide initiative after last year's graduating seniors averaged twenty-six unexcused absences. As Brit demonstrated, even that was easy enough to work around if you knew what to do.

The only poster in his room said, "It doesn't matter how good you are if you don't make the effort to show up." The poster showed two kittens lying in a sunbeam. Suzanne wondered what the kittens signified.

Brit smiled sweetly, trying her best to look innocent. It almost worked, but something about the black nail polish and the fraying Ramones shirt suggested she wasn't entirely on the level.

Suzanne saw Mr. Wells weighing whether or not to

pursue the matter further, but in the end, his apathy won out.

"Just make sure it's mine before giving me another heart attack, okay?"

Brit nodded. "Of course," she said, her face a mask of compliance.

Suzanne had to cough to cover her laughter.

The rest of homeroom was spent talking about Io.

"It's crazy how smooth you've got the controls," Mikayla said. "Like there's no lag between what I'm thinking and what my character does."

Their first few trips into the digital world had been marred by long loading times. One time, Mikayla's character froze and they had to all log out before the problem would go away.

"When are we gonna have a real fight?" Brit added. "I'm tired of kicking around goblins."

They chatted for a while about what bosses might be fun to take on before Mikayla whispered, "Does your dad know you're using the TII yet?"

Suzanne felt her stomach sink to her toes. "Sure,"

she said, but she could tell that Brit and Mikayla knew she was lying.

Mikayla frowned. "You've got to tell him."

"Why?" Brit said. "It's not like you tell your mom you spend all night gaming. And it's not like I tell my parents what I'm up to."

"That's completely different," Mikayla replied. "My mom would flip out if she knew the truth. I bet your dad would offer to help develop the game."

"Maybe," Suzanne said, but she knew that he wouldn't.

Her dad had shown her the first prototype for the TII when she was seven, right about the time he started teaching her how to write computer code. The TII, which stood for Total Immersion Interface, was designed as a psychiatric tool. Suzanne's dad explained that it ran on the same principles as REM sleep, but Suzanne still wasn't sure exactly what that meant. Still, she didn't need to know the nitty-gritty of how it worked. She just needed to know how to reprogram it.

The idea was that the TII would let a therapist enter into their patient's psyche by projecting a virtual reality version of the patient's subconscious. Suzanne still remembered the look of excitement on her parents' faces as they showed her around the tutorial program for the first time. Seven-year-old Suzanne immediately thought of using the TII as a gaming console.

"Maybe one day," her mom had said, smiling.

That was the only time Suzanne wore a TII until three years ago, the summer before her first year of high school. She found the three helmets in a box in the closet while she was looking for a backpack. Dusting them off, she was delighted to find that they still worked six years later.

She'd already been working on a fantasy RPG in her spare time, but she doubled her efforts once she discovered the TII. After a year of work, she had patched Io over to the TII and was ready to do beta testing. And who better to ask than her two best friends, Brit and Mikayla?

Something told her not to mention her new project to her dad. Maybe it was because she knew he had built the TII together with her mother and that anything to do with her was still a sore subject. Maybe it was because she no longer felt comfortable telling him everything. But whatever it was that held her back, she felt like telling him now, after years of secrecy, would only intensify how hurt and betrayed he would feel.

"Hello? Earth to Suze?"

Brit was waving her hand in front of Suzanne's face.

"Sorry," Suzanne said. "Got lost in my own head."

"What else is new?" Brit replied as the bell rang.

Chapter 3

Classes were never hard for Suzanne. In fact, she generally used her first two periods of the day to catch up on sleep. This isn't to say her school day was a breeze; it was just that she never worried about things like pop quizzes or extra homework. No, what bothered her during the school day wasn't so much a matter of what as it was a matter of whom.

This particular *whom* (who most people called Gretchen, with an emphasis on the "retch") had a daily mission to make Suzanne as miserable as possible. And so, as Suzanne walked with Mikayla back into Mr. Wells's classroom for their Intro to Technology class, her stomach did the usual nervous backflips. Intro to Tech was the only class she had with Gretchen. Gretchen tried to make every minute of the period count.

When she was nine and her parents still homeschooled her, Suzanne asked her dad to explain why baking soda and vinegar reacted the way they did. They spent the morning making a model volcano in the kitchen and then spent the afternoon cleaning it up. Her father said, "It's very complicated, but fundamentally they just don't get along." That's how Suzanne felt about Gretchen. On a fundamental level, she did not like Gretchen, and she knew Gretchen felt the same.

As evidenced by her delightful and imaginative nickname for Suzanne, "Suzandroid."

As in, "Hey Suzandroid, who are you going to homecoming with?"

Suzanne ignored her. Intro to Tech had assigned seating, so even though Mikayla was in the same class, she was stuck up at the front of the room where she couldn't help. Suzanne learned early on that the best tactic to take when dealing with Gretchen was to ignore her and hope she lost interest. This wasn't the easiest thing to do, as the seating chart isolated them in the back of the room, but Suzanne had plenty of practice ignoring whatever Gretchen said.

"What kind of dress did you get, Suzandroid?"

Ignore her, Suzanne told herself. She checked the clock on her computer—only thirty minutes until class ended. She could make it.

Unfortunately, Gretchen seemed unusually motivated today.

Suzanne heard the scrape of chair legs on linoleum. Horrified, she turned to see Gretchen walking towards her at a surprising speed, considering how high Gretchen's heels were.

Gretchen was, in many ways, everything Suzanne was not. It seemed that she had a new outfit every day, all of which looked like they'd been cut out of a magazine. Suzanne sometimes worn the same sweatpants every day for a week. Like Mikayla, Gretchen was a captain on the cheer squad. Unlike Mikayla, she abused practically every privilege that granted her.

Gretchen deposited her handbag on the desk next to Suzanne's and lowered herself into the seat.

"Are you going to Kyle's after-party?" she asked, without a hint of sarcasm.

"No," Suzanne replied flatly, "I'm not going."

"What?" Gretchen replied, pretending to be scandalized. "But it won't be any fun without you! Everyone's going to be there."

"I wasn't invited." Sometimes, if Suzanne admitted how unpopular she was up front, Gretchen would be satisfied and leave her alone. No such luck today.

"That must have been a mistake. I'll find you at the dance and we'll go over together."

"I'm not going to the dance," said Suzanne quietly.

"But why not?" Gretchen asked, her voice incredulous. Suzanne wondered if she had ever considered acting.

"It's not really my thing. I don't think I'll have fun."

"Well, if you'd rather stay home alone," Gretchen began. She didn't have to finish the sentence. Most of the kids in the class were staring at the back of the room now, drawn to their conversation. Gretchen was a master of whispering loud enough for entire classrooms to hear.

"Is it because no one asked you?" Gretchen continued in her stage whisper. "That's the reason, isn't it?"

"Sure," Suzanne said weakly. She looked to the front of the room, but Mr. Wells was completely engrossed in his computer, headphones blasting music into his ears. That had to be against some regulation.

"Well, that's just rude." Gretchen flashed Suzanne a smile, as if an idea had suddenly come to her. "I know! Why don't you ask someone?"

Suzanne scowled at Gretchen who kept smiling blithely.

"It's a big school. Someone must be desperate enough to go with you."

Some of the boys sitting closest to them laughed. Suzanne felt her face growing hot and she looked down. She knew they were just bored. Some would even approach her later and half-mumble apologies, forcing Suzanne to suffer the indignity of having to forgive them. She was sick of forgiving people for laughing at her, she was sick of getting bullied every day, and, most of all, she was sick of Gretchen.

"Hey, Gretch? Shut up."

Suzanne looked up and saw Mikayla turned around in her seat.

"Maybe if you actually paid attention in class instead of being such a bitch all the time you wouldn't have to keep repeating classes."

It was a well known but little acknowledged fact that Gretchen's academics were the weak point in her performance at Perry Hall High School. Several kids let out low *Oooooh*'s and the same boys who had laughed at Suzanne moments ago now chuckled at Gretchen's expense.

The smile melted off of Gretchen's face.

"Was I talking to you?" she asked.

"Well, you were talking so loud I had to assume," Mikayla retorted.

Suzanne watched the spat with wonder. One of the sacred laws of the cheer squad was squadmates were never allowed to fight in public. Coach Foster claimed this was bad for morale. A united team meant united cheers. Coach hated cracks in her pyramid.

Suzanne felt a surge of gratitude for her friend. From what Mikayla had told her of squad practices (breaking another sacred law, never to reveal secrets to outsiders) Gretchen was just as horrible when practicing handsprings as she was in Intro to Tech. But Gretchen was always wary of Mikayla, because they were co-captains, and because Mikayla was as widely liked as Gretchen was despised.

Before the confrontation turned physical something incredible happened. Mr. Wells stood up and cleared his throat. The students, surprised to see him exercise his authority, instantly fell silent.

Flustered by their obedience, Mr. Wells cleared his throat again. Then, he looked at Gretchen, and said one word. "Detention."

"Excuse me?"

"I'm going to give you detention, Gretchen." He looked as surprised as she did.

"Mr. Wells," she began, but he cut her off.

"No. Stop talking or you'll get more detention. A, um, week more of detention. Starting tomorrow."

Suzanne could barely believe what she was hearing. Mikayla flashed her a smile from the front of the room.

Gretchen was on her feet, protesting. "It wasn't even my fault! I was just asking Suzanne for some help on the final project, but she was working on her own thing so we started talking about who we were going to the dance with!"

"Oh, come on," Suzanne said before she could stop herself.

Gretchen turned angrily towards her but Mr. Wells waved her off.

"Enough. One day of detention Gretchen. Everybody go back to your assigned seats. I want you all to work silently for the rest of the class. Anybody who talks will be joining Gretchen here after school."

Gretchen stalked back to her seat. Suzanne had been compiling code for her game instead of working on her final, but she saved the program and pretended to do work for the rest of the period. She saw Gretchen glaring at her from across the room and could only imagine what new torments there would be for her tomorrow. At least she was safe for the rest of class. Now she only had the rest of high school to worry about.

Chapter 4

When Brit heard what had happened in Intro to Tech that day, she laughed until she snorted. They were in Suzanne's room, waiting for the TII to finish installing the patch Suzanne had written that day.

"I'd give anything to see the look on her face," she chuckled, wiping a tear from her eye.

Suzanne laughed too, but Mikayla had an uneasy look on her face. She was still wearing her cheer squad outfit, albeit now with sweatpants. "I'm just waiting to see how she gets back at me. You know she's already planning something."

"Way to be a buzzkill," Brit said. She was sitting

on Suzanne's beanbag. Suzanne got too tall for the beanbag chair when she was in junior high, but Brit was so short that she still fit. "Come on! You just took the queen bitch down! That's gotta be what, a hundred XP?"

"At least," Suzanne said.

"Don't get me wrong," Mikayla said. "You don't know how nice it was practicing without her. Nobody cried today. That was a first."

They all laughed at that. The computer chimed, which meant the game was ready.

"Finally!" Suzanne said, booting up the program. "Come on, let's fire it up."

"What did you change?" Mikayla asked, picking up one of the TII helmets.

Suzanne smiled coyly. "Some graphics bugs. A couple of attack animations. Other small stuff. You'll see." She was bursting to give away the surprise but she didn't want to ruin it. The code she had compiled during Intro to Tech was the last bit of the game's full beta. Today, they were going to leave the Meadow of Beginnings and enter Io proper.

But Brit and Mikayla didn't know that. Right as they finished putting their helmets on Suzanne heard a knock on her door. It had to be her dad, saying goodnight before he went out to his gig as a security guard. He had more degrees than could fit on a business card, but he was spending his nights watching over empty campus buildings at the nearby college.

"We doing this or what?" Brit's voice was muffled by the TII.

"Give me a minute," Suzanne said. She slipped out into the hallway so her dad wouldn't see them using his invention.

Much to her surprise, he was clean shaven.

"I'm about to head out, sweetie," he said. "You want me to get you anything while I'm gone?"

"No thanks," she said. "I'll be asleep when you get back." That was only sort of a lie; in the TII she might as well have been asleep. Her body acted like she was dreaming.

He lingered in the hallway with a guilty look on his face. "I'm going out of town this weekend," he said. Suzanne was shocked. Her dad never went out of town. He worked weekend nights.

"I've got a job interview. You remember my buddy from grad school, Mike?"

Suzanne shook her head, dumbfounded. As far as she knew her dad didn't have any friends. He wasn't what you would call social.

"Well, he has a company up in Jersey, and it's expanding, and he's looking for a project manager. So he asked me if I was interested. It's a lot more money and . . . "

He trailed off, looking around the apartment. Suzanne never minded how small it was; it was enough space for the two of them. And besides, it was where they had lived when her mom was still alive.

Her dad seemed to feel differently. He never called the apartment home. It was always "the apartment" or "the place we're renting."

"It's a lot more money," he repeated.

"Wait," Suzanne said. "If Mike's company is in New Jersey, does that mean we're going to move?"

Her dad looked even more uncomfortable. "If I take the job," he said.

"If you take the job." The prospect of starting over at a new school made the words sound hollow in her mouth.

"Let's talk about this later," her dad said, forcing a smile. He kissed her on the forehead, muttered another "Bye" and was out the door.

"What was that about?" Mikayla asked when Suzanne returned to her room. That was just like Mikayla to worry over everything, but right now Suzanne just wanted to log into another reality.

"Nothing," she said. Suzanne suddenly imagined starting over at a new school, without Brit or Mikayla. No doubt there were plenty of Gretchens in Jersey.

So the session started off on a particularly dour note. But whatever problems the girls were facing in the real world, Io provided a limitless set of distractions. It was hard to worry about moving or Gretchen when goblins were trying to stab you.

By the time they made it to the end of the

42

Meadow of Beginnings, Suzanne had forgotten all about her dad's job interview.

Mikayla slew Igor Redcap this play through, gaining a level in the process. Suzanne watched as Mikayla's character was immersed in golden light. Mikayla stared straight ahead, her eyes focusing on something only she could see. Suzanne knew that Mikayla was looking at her stat increases. Mikayla read off her new stats and Suzanne checked them against what she expected for a level six Ranger.

But instead of a loot drop appearing as Igor's body dissipated, a closed door appeared in its place.

"What's that?" Brit asked, jogging to catch up to the other girls. She'd gotten held up dealing with the Mages again. Despite Suzanne's advice, Brit insisted on playing as a Fighter, a class that focused on offense and offered little in the way of resisting magic spells.

"That's the door to the rest of the world," Suzanne said.

The other girls gasped.

Suzanne made a sweeping gesture with her arm

that she hoped was grand. "Today you'll see the rest of Io."

The door swung open. Before them the Meadow ended and a whole world waited.

Through the door, what Suzanne saw stretched for miles. The Meadow sat atop a tall plateau. The cliff face dropped off into a wide valley. A huge road stretched the length of the valley, connecting a series of small towns.

Other settlements were scattered across the landscape. Some were hidden away in forests and others sat prominently on the peaks of hills. Smaller pathways connected them to each other and to the main road.

The road stretched south, passing through a forest to a swampy fenland at the edge of the map. To the north, rocky outcroppings sprang from the ground, eventually giving way to mountains. And far off to the west, on the other side of the valley, Suzanne could see a mighty river, far wider than any in the real world.

"Wow," Mikayla said.

'Wow' doesn't do it justice, Suzanne thought. This

was Io. This was her world. Not just lines of code or a map on a screen, but a playable, livable virtual reality.

Staring closely at the road, Suzanne could see small clouds of dust traveling north. She felt a thrill of excitement as she realized the clouds were NPCs—non-player characters—traveling of their own accord.

Suzanne hadn't built all these towns. She'd laid the groundwork for Io's two kingdoms, designing the terrain for Pyxis and Altair, and had built their capital cities. But she hadn't done much else besides that on the map front. Instead, she had built the game's artificial intelligence.

The AI animated all of the NPCs. Following real-world time, the world of Io was barely months old. But in game time it had existed for centuries, more than enough time for settlements to develop organically within her constraints.

Every town had to have an inn where the girls could rest and recover HP. And towns were protected areas; as long as they were occupied, monsters couldn't cross the threshold into them.

Suzanne mandated the existence of some other

places, like the dungeons for bosses. Those she had designed herself. But besides that, Io was as new to her as it was to Brit and Mikayla.

"What are we waiting for?" Suzanne asked, walking through the door. Brit and Mikayla followed her. Together the three of them began the descent down to the valley and the rest of the virtual world.

The way down the side of the plateau was almost without incident. The girls had a brief skirmish with a roc—a giant eagle with metal claws—after Brit trampled its nest. A few quick slashes from Mikayla's blade convinced the bird to look for easier prey. It flew back up the mountainside, squawking in anger. But because Mikayla didn't finish the bird off, the girls didn't get any loot from the battle, or any XP.

Brit shouted insults at the retreating roc, but that was all she could hit it with. Suzanne's throwing daggers were the only ranged weapons their party had. Mikayla could spend Energite to launch Wind Slashes from her sword, but the roc wasn't worth the effort.

"Leave it," Suzanne said. "I want to find some NPCs!"

She wondered how the NPCs would act. The AI was supposed to select a few out of every area and give them deeper personalities. The others were supposed to recite a couple of repeatable lines of dialogue. Suzanne filled the dialogue engine with the script of every RPG she could find from which the engine produced new sentences. If everything worked out, the NPCs wouldn't just spout gibberish.

She didn't have to wait long. Half an hour's walk from the base of the plateau was a small town called Oppold. Oppold consisted of a dozen homes and a scattering of small businesses, like a smith and an inn.

The homes were all small cottages, clustered around the town square. The cottages all had the same rough blueprints: wooden walls with thatched roofs. They weren't much to look at, but Suzanne could hardly contain her excitement. She ran up to them, knocking on their walls, fingering the roofing.

"It's a village!" she practically shouted. NPCs gave odd stares and hurried their children away.

"Play it cool," Mikayla hissed. "You're scaring them."

That barely mattered to Suzanne. She could hardly believe what she was seeing. Sure, the cottages all looked fairly similar, but they were still cottages! Presumably filled with families! Families of all kinds! All generated by the code she had written. It was too much for her to take in at once.

"Seriously, you look like you're about to have a seizure," Brit said.

Suzanne did her best to calm down. The NPCs, after another moment of interest, resumed their business. Each one of them, regardless of class, gender, or appearance, was marked by a gray diamond twirling over their head, just like the red diamonds that twirled over monsters and the bright green diamonds twirling over each of the girls. She could tell they were all Citizens, the standard villager class, from the way they were dressed. Citizens didn't wear armor and didn't fight. Mostly they were there so the player characters could get quests and buy items. Still, even among Citizens, there were dozens of different NPC appearances, and that was just in this one small town.

"This is nuts," Suzanne said. "This is the coolest thing ever."

Mikayla and Brit thought it was awesome, but they didn't want to just stare at NPCs. They walked off to see if any of the merchants were selling anything worth spending their gold on. They came back an hour later. Suzanne was still sitting in the town square, staring at NPCs.

As they walked up, the blinking 6:30 A.M. appeared in the sky.

"You moved the alarm up," Mikayla noted.

Suzanne pulled her attention away from the NPCs. "Yeah. We can't keep showing up late, right?"

"What do we do?" Brit said. "Log out like usual?"

"We have to go to sleep," Suzanne said. "Let's head to the inn."

The sign hanging over the inn read, THE BELCHING MINOTAUR. A cartoon image of a

Minotaur burping vigorously was painted below the name.

But after they went inside, the name of the inn was hardly the most ridiculous thing about it.

"That's insane! Who charges five hundred gold for a room?" Brit demanded. Each time the girls killed Igor Redcap and all his goblins they got one hundred and fifty gold total.

The innkeeper at the Belching Minotaur apparently did. He was not a Minotaur, but an elderly human NPC. His face was lined with age and he leaned heavily on a stick for support. Two ornery tufts of hair as gray as the diamond twirling above his head sprouted above his ears.

"If you don't like it, you can take your business elsewhere," he grumbled. "Course, I'm the only inn roundabouts, so that won't get you too far."

Suzanne was tempted to wipe the smug look off the innkeeper's face, but she knew better than to pick a fight with random NPCs. She wanted to test out her new world and beating up surly innkeepers wasn't going to give her any usable data.

"Let me handle this," she said. Brit was red in the face and gripping her halberd like she intended to use it.

"What my friend is trying to say is that those prices seem a little steep. Any chance we could work out some kind of deal?"

The innkeeper's eyes went from Suzanne's face to the daggers thrust through her belt, to Mikayla's sheathed sword, to the halberd clutched in Brit's hand.

"Where you lot from?" he asked.

"The East," Suzanne said, which was technically true. They had walked west from the Meadow of Beginnings to reach Oppold.

"Where East?" The innkeeper regarded the three of them with suspicion. He looked as worn out as the rest of the town, dressed in ratty trousers and a patchy vest. "This is the end of the road."

"Look," Mikayla said, interrupting. "We need a place to stay for the night. Is five hundred really the lowest you're willing to go?"

The innkeeper put a finger to his mouth like he was considering. "Yes," he said. "Like I said, it's the end of the road here. Not a lot of travelers coming through these days. Got to make ends meet, don't I?"

Mikayla sighed and motioned the girls away from the bar. "We've got the money," she said. "Why don't we just pay it?"

Brit was scandalized.

"Are you nuts? That's basically all our gold. How are we going to buy better shit?"

"Where were you thinking of shopping?" Mikayla retorted. "None of the merchants were open, in case you didn't notice, and the forge was closed down."

That struck Suzanne as odd. The merchants were supposed to be buying and selling in every town, regardless of size. Still, if one town was without commerce that was no big deal.

"We should just pay him," Suzanne reasoned. "We've got to get to school anyway. And besides, we want to test things out as much as possible."

Brit snorted with disgust but she kept quiet as Mikayla handed over the gold to the innkeeper.

"Thank you kindly." He pointed up the stairs. "Room's on the left. Can't miss it, it's the only one."

Suddenly, a little boy burst through the door of the inn, with what looked like a bit of rope clutched in his hand. He stared for a second at the girls, awed by their armor. Collecting himself, he dove beneath a table. The innkeeper let out a long sigh.

A second later the door was flung open again, this time by an adolescent girl. Her face was the picture of fury. Her hair looked as if it had been done up in pigtails, but one of her braids was missing.

"Where is he?"

"Haven't seen him," the innkeeper said.

The ruse might have worked. Brit stood in the way of the table, blocking the hiding boy from the girl's view. But he giggled so loudly that she figured out where he was in a matter of seconds.

She grabbed him by the ankle and began dragging him out from under the table. The boy's eyes widened with fear as he tried to kick her hands away.

"Help me!" he pleaded, beseeching Brit.

Brit looked down at him stone-faced. "Nah, dude," she said. "Looks like you deserve this one."

He wailed in terror and kicked harder than ever.

"Enough!" the innkeeper shouted, banging his gnarled hand on the counter. Immediately the girl let go of the boy's leg and the boy stopped kicking. But then the girl kicked him, hard.

He stood up clutching his bottom. "Grandpa!" he said. "Henny kicked me!"

"That she did," the innkeeper replied. "Be glad she didn't do worse."

The little boy scowled.

"Make him give it back," Henny said.

"Give it back, Ib."

"Ain't gonna," the little boy said. He held the severed braid aloft. Turning, he tossed it into the fire.

Suzanne, Brit, Mikayla, and Henny watched as the fire reduced the braid to cinders. Ib took the opportunity to dart out the door into the evening. Henny paused to wail in anger before chasing after him.

"Them kids," the innkeeper said. Suzanne noticed a misty look in his eyes.

"They'll grow out of it," Brit said. "You should've seen me at his age."

The innkeeper smiled. "Were you this big then?"

Suzanne almost laughed. In the real world, Brit wasn't even five feet tall. But in the game, Brit was a Fighter, and as a result her character towered over the other girls. She had to duck under the doorway of the Belching Minotaur when they entered.

"Just about," she said.

"Heh. Then I'd hate to have been your folks."

Suzanne saw Brit squirm at the remark. "Come on," Suzanne said, beckoning to Brit and Mikayla. "We need to crash."

Saying goodnight to the innkeeper, they tramped upstairs. Their room was barren except for three cots. A single window let in pale moonlight from outside.

"Yeah, this was totally worth all our gold," Brit muttered. She stuck her armor in her inventory and threw herself onto one of the cots. With her armor off, her character was dressed in nondescript leather clothes. They didn't offer much in the way of padding.

"Ow, shit!" she said. "What the fuck is wrong with this bed?"

Suzanne tried her cot, a little more carefully than Brit had. But there was no doubt about it; it was the least comfortable surface she had ever felt.

Mikayla lay down gingerly, shifting a little to try and find a more comfortable position.

"I guess the NPCs don't care about how comfortable beds are."

Suzanne tried lying on her back, her stomach and both shoulders, but no matter how she did it she couldn't get comfortable.

"We should invent real beds," Brit said. "I bet we'd make a fortune."

"That wouldn't be too hard," Suzanne said. "We'd just have to find some straw or something."

"Let's revolutionize the mattress market tomorrow," Mikayla said. "We've got to get to homeroom."

Suzanne leaned back onto the bed and closed her eyes. Just as she had planned, the game world shrank down into a pixel. In a matter of minutes she was sitting up on her real bed, pulling her helmet off and getting ready to face reality.

Chapter 5

Suzanne sleepwalked through the next morning at school. Her last class before lunch was history, which was the only class she shared with Brit, and the teacher, Mr. McDougal, surprised them with a multiple-choice quiz. Suzanne finished hers, and then, as was their custom, faked a sneeze and sent her paper gliding to the floor. Brit picked it up, memorizing Suzanne's answers before handing it back. As Suzanne turned in her quiz, Brit copied the answers down, changing one or two so she'd get a lower score.

On principle, Suzanne disapproved of cheating, but she quickly realized pretty much everyone was doing it. Kids searched for the right answers on their smart phones or hid crib notes up the sleeves of their sweatshirts. The most brazen simply kept the textbook open in their laps. Due to a combination of the students' initiative and the teachers' laziness, hardly anyone ever got caught.

In fact, Suzanne and Brit became friends directly because of cheating. They were in their freshmen biology class and they were supposed to be labeling the parts of an eye. Suzanne finished first and was about to turn in her work when she felt someone tap on her shoulder.

She turned around to see Brit trying to copy off her worksheet.

"Just give me one more second," Brit whispered. "I'm almost done."

Suzanne was indignant. Before she'd started at public schools, her dad sat her down and gave her a huge talk about life at school. Part of that involved other students. He skimped on how to handle bullies, but made sure that she knew that cheating was wrong. She promised never to cheat, but her dad never said anything about letting other kids copy off of her work.

Something about Brit's manner left her uncertain. So she waited until Brit filled in the last answer, *viscous fluid*, and then she turned the worksheet in.

After class, Brit caught up to her in the hallway.

"I'm Brit," and she stuck out her hand to shake.

Suzanne took it timidly. "Suzanne," she said.

"Thanks a bunch, Suze. You're a real lifesaver."

She dashed off, leaving Suzanne confused and conflicted.

Later that day was gym, the class Suzanne dreaded the most. Suzanne had never played sports as a child, her parents preferring science projects to soccer practice, and the idea of showering in a room full of girls she had never met before terrified her. She was quivering in the locker room when Brit dropped down on the bench besides her.

"You're new, huh?"

Suzanne managed a nod.

"Whatever you do, don't look the teacher in the

eye. And say *ma'am* at the end of every sentence, okay?"

Suzanne nodded again. During that class she followed Brit's instructions, and managed to escape without having to run the additional laps the coach assigned, "to teach you punks some manners."

After that, Brit took Suzanne under her wing. Not long after they became friends, Gretchen began her tormenting. Brit kept Gretchen and her cronies from trying anything in the hallways. Even if Suzanne wouldn't break rules, Brit pushed her to bend them, like convincing Suzanne to use the Intro to Tech computers for her own projects.

Once Suzanne tried to explain to Brit that they had a symbiotic relationship, but Brit had a better word for it.

"We're friends," she said. It was as simple as that. Brit was over at Suzanne's place, checking out the earliest versions of Io.

"I know," Suzanne said. "I just . . . "

She didn't know how to voice her concerns. She worried that Brit was her friend for grades and she worried that telling Brit her suspicions would end the friendship immediately.

Brit caught her meaning.

"Look," she said. "I'm not just friends with you to pass bio."

Suzanne felt ashamed she had even thought of it.

"I'm friends with you so I can come over here and play video games."

The girls both broke out laughing, but Brit was only half-kidding. The one time Suzanne went over to Brit's house was shocking. Everything in Brit's room was soft, fluffy, and pink.

Brit looked around her room, shrugged, and said, "My mom decorated it."

When Suzanne met Brit's mom, she was even more surprised. Brit's mother went on a tangent against video games because they, "rotted young minds," and "encouraged unladylike behavior." Her rant also touched on other reprehensible behaviors like chewing with one's mouth open or speaking one's mind. After that they only hung out at Suzanne's so they could, as Brit said, play games.

Suzanne was halfway through explaining the controls when her buzzer rang.

"That must be Mikayla!" Brit said.

Who? Suzanne wondered. By the time she realized that Brit had invited someone over without asking, Brit was already opening the door.

Suzanne's first impression of Mikayla was that there was no way she and Brit were friends. Mikayla, to put it bluntly, looked popular. Suzanne didn't have another word for it. Even though they were still freshmen, Mikayla had all the poise of an upperclassman. Suzanne had seen her in the school hallways, immersed in a crowd of people. Mikayla was even wearing a cheerleader's uniform to complete the popular-girl stereotype.

Mikayla explained she had come straight from practice and hadn't had time to change. Brit had been raving to her about "Some super-genius new kid who had built her own video game."

"So what's this game?" she asked after introducing herself.

Surprised, Suzanne showed her.

They spent the afternoon going through an early version of the Meadow of Beginnings. Over the next two years they tested the game as much as possible. It was only last summer that Suzanne showed the other girls the TII.

Brit and Mikayla didn't believe what Suzanne was describing at first. Brit kept starting questions and not finishing them, and Mikayla was sitting silent on Suzanne's bed, staring at a TII helmet.

Brit said, "So you're telling me that your parents invented a . . . "

"A TII," Suzanne offered.

" . . . A TII that puts people inside video games, and it's powered by dreams?"

Suzanne laughed. "It isn't powered by dreams. It just runs off the same principle as REM sleep."

But she avoided trying to explain too much. In all honesty, she wasn't entirely sure how the TII worked herself.

Brit wasn't convinced.

"Don't you think if they had invented something

like that, you guys would be rich? Like Bill Gates money."

Mikayla looked up from the TII and stared at Suzanne.

"Let's just do the demo," Suzanne said.

"I mean, come on," Brit continued. She was about to say more, but Mikayla put a hand on her shoulder.

"Is it safe?" Mikayla asked.

"Yeah," Suzanne said, "as safe as dreaming."

"You're one-hundred percent sure?"

"Positive," Suzanne lied.

"Then who cares how it works?" Mikayla said. "I want to try it out."

Suzanne instructed them to put their helmets on, and a minute later, they were in the demo level.

The first hurdle they had to overcome was movement.

"Stop thinking of your character's body as your body," Suzanne suggested. "Try to imagine you're using a controller. Don't walk—move forwards."

Her advice helped. It had taken Suzanne three

separate trips into the TII to figure out how to move on her own. With her help, Brit and Mikayla picked it up in an hour of in-game time.

Soon they were abusing the modified physics of the tutorial program to run on walls and otherwise ignore gravity. Not long after that, the girls made their characters. Suzanne put her previous character, an overpowered Assassin, in a save file. Maybe she would pull her back out one day, but it made more sense to grow a new character alongside Brit and Mikayla.

When Suzanne told the girls it was time to log out, they did so with great reluctance. Brit spent the rest of that afternoon exclaiming over the invention. Mikayla, shocked speechless, nodded along like a bobblehead. All Suzanne remembered from that day was an overwhelming sense of validation.

✳

The reminiscence carried her through the rest of

history. When the bell rang she filed out of the classroom, pausing to copy down that night's reading into her phone's calendar. She found Brit in the hallway, and together they went to lunch.

Normally their school let them sit out on the lawn for lunch, but it was raining so hard everyone crammed into the cafeteria. The girls squeezed into a single table with what looked like the entire pep band, and had to shout to hear themselves over the noise in the crowded cafeteria.

"That quiz was easy," Brit yelled.

"Sure it was," Mikayla said. She dropped her voice. "Be honest. How many answers did Suzanne give you?"

"All of them," Suzanne replied.

Mikayla gave Brit a look. "What?" Brit said, shrugging. "Some kids have brains and some kids have friends."

"And what do you have?" Mikayla teased.

"What's got you in such a good mood?" Brit asked.

"Gretchen wasn't in French today. Which means

she won't be at two practices in a row! Truly a blessed occasion."

Suzanne yawned. She couldn't keep pulling all-nighters like this or she would be sleeping in her casserole.

All of a sudden the lunch room fell deathly silent. That could only mean one thing: a teacher had entered, one of the hard-asses.

Suzanne craned her neck and saw Coach Foster stalking across the lunchroom. Students scattered to give her a wide berth. Even those not on the cheer squad had to suffer through gym class with Coach, an experience better measured by lumps and bruises than by conventional letter grades.

Coach Foster was headed right their way. She looked like a soldier ready for battle, complete with a helmet of chrome hair. Her hair never moved. Suzanne wondered what percentage of it was hair-spray. As the coach approached, she considered hiding under the table.

Before Suzanne could duck for cover, the pep

band fell silent and scooted towards the other end of the table. Coach Foster had arrived.

"So," Coach said to Mikayla. "I hear you don't value teamwork."

Mikayla stuttered a few syllables. Coach Foster snorted in disgust.

"To be honest, Watkins, it's only your considerable talent that's kept you on the squad. I've had misgivings about your attitude since you tried out."

The terrified Mikayla hung her head in shame.

"Do you know what I'm talking about, Watkins?"

Mikayla shook her head.

"Smith missed practice yesterday, and now Monsieur DuPont informs me she's out sick today as well. Her mother called the school and reported she was being bullied. Apparently you can't handle being co-captains."

Mikayla opened her mouth but no words came out. No matter what the Coach said, Suzanne knew Mikayla would never talk back.

"Effective immediately, you are the squad's new

equipment manager. Maybe cleaning up after your squadmates will teach you to respect their feelings."

And with that, the coach stalked off.

No one spoke for a few minutes. Eventually the pep band stopped staring and resumed their engrossing debate over reed sizes.

Mikayla was visibly shaken. Suzanne could imagine the lies Gretchen had told Coach Foster. Something in Gretchen's ruthless attitude appealed to the coach.

Finally, Brit spoke. "What a bitch."

Suzanne nodded. "Do you mean the coach or Gretchen?"

Mikayla laughed, but it sounded more like she was choking. She put her elbows on the table and her head in her hands.

"This is going to suck. This is going to suck so hard."

"You could always quit?" Suzanne suggested.

Brit motioned for her to zip it, but it was too late. Mikayla glared at Suzanne.

"Not all of us can count on a perfect GPA to get us into college."

Even though she knew Mikayla didn't mean it, the jab still hurt. Mikayla hastily apologized.

"Sorry. It's just that there's no way I can get back at Gretchen. She's got Coach wrapped around her little finger."

A mischievous smile appeared on Brit's face. "You want to get back at her, huh? Leave that to me."

"Oh no," Mikayla said. Both she and Suzanne knew that smile all too well. It was a signal that Brit was up to no good. The last time they had seen it, all the fire alarms in school mysteriously went off during finals.

Brit patted Mikayla on the wrist. "Don't worry. You don't know anything. Just wait to see what happens when Gretchen comes back to school."

And with that, she walked out of the cafeteria, still smiling that mischievous smile.

Chapter 6

They skipped out on Io that evening because Mikayla had a game. The next day was a half day. School only lasted half as long, and as a result, half the student body decided to skip. Suzanne basically slept through her classes, rushing back to her place with Mikayla when school was over.

Brit was sitting in the courtyard of Suzanne's building, waiting for them.

"Did I miss anything good?" she asked.

"All our finals were canceled and I was voted prom queen," Suzanne said.

"You were voted prom queen? Now I know you're lying."

Suzanne was in too good of a mood to care what Brit said. They had the whole afternoon and all of that night to play in Io.

"Come on," she said. "Let's go game."

She pulled on the TII. The game loaded with her in bed in the Belching Minotaur. Henny, the one-braided NPC, was smacking her in the face.

"Wha?" Suzanne muttered, struggling upright.

"They got Gramps!" the little girl shouted. "You gotta help!" And just for good measure, she smacked Suzanne again.

Suzanne pushed Henny off. The NPC fell to the floor. Immediately, she was up and trying to shake Brit and Mikayla awake as well. While Suzanne equipped her gear, she tried to puzzle out what the girl meant. She thought she had paused the game while their characters were asleep, but apparently, events had progressed.

While the other girls fully logged in and their characters woke up, Suzanne withdrew her equipment from her inventory. Unlike Brit, who played as a Fighter, Suzanne was a Rogue. Her class wasn't as physically strong as Brit's, but it was much faster. She fought primarily with daggers and cunning, wearing light armor to facilitate easier movement.

In another minute Brit and Mikayla were up and dressed.

"Who's got your grandpa?" Mikayla asked, strapping on her sword belt.

"The Mongrels!" Henny whimpered, her eyes wide with fear. Now that she had managed to get the girls up, she didn't seem to know what to do with herself next. Dropping cross-legged to the ground, she began to cry.

"We've got to check this out," Mikayla said. She hesitated, unsure of how to proceed.

"You two go out the front," Suzanne said. "I'm going to get vantage from the roof."

Before they could respond, she opened the window and went out. Balancing on the narrow ledge, she reached up for the roof. The first tile she grabbed came loose and fell a story to the ground below. Teetering to regain her balance, Suzanne grabbed again. This time the tile held and she pulled herself up to the roof.

She saw an Archer perched on the rooftop, bow drawn. Suzanne stayed low as she crept forward. One of the class bonuses for Rogues gave them a stealth advantage, so the Archer didn't notice her. Besides, all of his attention was focused on his target: the innkeeper.

Not that the innkeeper was going anywhere. His arms were bound behind his back and he was lying on his side. Standing with a foot on the innkeeper's chest was a Berserker, his axe drawn. An ugly scar, drawn from the top of his left ear across to the right side of his mouth split his face into a cruel sneer.

"Peasants!" the Berserker roared. "We, the Mongrels, have no desire for more bloodshed. Have you not suffered enough at our hands?"

To emphasize his point he stomped down on the innkeeper, who whimpered, and muttered something. Whatever it was amused the Berserker terribly; he laughed as he kicked the innkeeper in the ribs.

The Archer perched on the rooftop chuckled

nastily at the scene. Suzanne almost laughed herself. The AI was generating all of the conflict by itself! Her game worked!

She ached to start the fight and see what it was like battling NPCs, but she didn't want to get sniped from another roof. She checked the other rooftops; they were clear of enemies.

Flames and smoke were pouring out of some of the cottages and the villagers of Oppold were huddled in the town square. Two Barbarians and a Sellsword kept them under guard while the Berserker put on his display. Suzanne saw Ib, the innkeeper's grandson, staring out from among the villagers, concern stamped on his young face. Red diamonds twirled over the heads of the classed characters, with a red crown floating above the Berserker. That confirmed the Mongrels as enemies and the Berserker as their boss.

"Give us your gold and your Energite crystals," the Berserker commanded. "And some of you might live to have the pleasure of us raiding you again."

His speech was cut short as Brit burst from the inn, Mikayla a step behind her.

The Berserker didn't flinch. Speaking to the villagers, he said, "These girlies are the best you've got? They're hardly worth dirtying my axe over. At least the bunch before were worth a scrap."

Looking directly at Brit and Mikayla, he chuckled. "Come on, girlies. No need to waste such pretty faces."

"Gross," Mikayla said, drawing her sword. Despite what she said, Suzanne saw Mikayla was amped up for the fight.

Brit nodded. "Do you think he fights as well as he monologues?"

"Big talk for such a little girlie," the Berserker smirked.

Then a few things happened at once. The Berserker looked up. Suzanne realized this was a signal to the Archer, whose aim shifted to the back of Mikayla's head. Before the Archer could loose a shot, Suzanne had a dagger around his throat.

"Try it," she whispered, edging the Archer forward

so one of his feet dangled over the edge of the roof. Suzanne felt the NPC gulp in fear. She felt it!

While that happened, Mikayla launched herself at the Mongrels guarding the villagers. They turned from the NPCs, ready to engage.

When the Berserker looked up, Brit slammed the pole of her halberd into his nuts. A look of surprise and fury replaced the smirk as the armored man dropped his axe and held his crotch with both hands.

"Big armor for such a little man," Brit said. While the Berserker was still clutching his privates, she spun and slammed the blade of her halberd into his back.

Suzanne saw Mikayla disarm one of the Barbarians; with a quick parry, she sent the other stumbling towards the inn.

Suzanne let the Archer go. The bowman landed on the Barbarian and both collapsed in a heap. Mikayla looked up to the rooftop and smiled at Suzanne.

The disarmed Barbarian took the opportunity to tackle Mikayla. Suzanne cursed, realizing she was now useless up on the roof. The Barbarian nearly had Mikayla pinned when Brit grabbed him by the shoulders and hurled him across the town square into a burning cottage.

The Sellsword grabbed Ib and held his blade up to the boy's throat.

"Don't you move," he said in a panicked voice. "I'll do it, I swear."

Brit and Mikayla froze. Suzanne wanted to shout, "He's just an NPC!" But it was hard not to get caught up in the game, hard not to play along.

"Tell your friend to come down from the roof," the Sellsword continued. Suzanne lowered herself down and walked over to Brit and Mikayla.

The Sellsword looked around at the other Mongrels, who were beginning to pick themselves up off the ground. "Now here's what's going to happen," he started.

But then Ib bit him on the hand. Shouting in pain, the Sellsword dropped the child. Mikayla cuffed him in the head with her shield. A dazed expression came over his face and he collapsed on the ground.

Brit and Mikayla high-fived.

"Oh shit," Suzanne said. The Berserker was getting up.

"Mongrels, to me!"

The Mongrels, or what remained of them, rallied around their leader. The Archer's bow had snapped and neither of the Barbarians had their weapons. From their inventories, they withdrew replacements. Clearly, they were used to drawn-out fights like this. Despite herself, Suzanne was impressed by the NPCs' foresight.

"Alright, girlies," the Berserker snapped. "Let's see how good you are in a fair fight."

"How is four on three fair?" replied Suzanne.

"And weren't you taking hostages a minute ago?" Mikayla asked.

Brit stepped forward. "Enough with this 'girlie' bullshit. We've got names, okay? Mine is Brit."

The Berserker barked a laugh. "Whatever they might have called you earlier, when I'm finished with you, they'll call you dead."

Brit rolled her eyes. "Tell me you didn't write that, Suze."

Suzanne blushed. "I'm still working on the dialogue algorithm," she whispered. "Can we just get these guys already?"

The Mongrels attacked. One of the Barbarians took a two-handed swing at Suzanne's neck, but she nimbly dodged backwards. Dancing forward she delivered a series of quick slashes to his chest and arms. Howling in pain, he dropped his hatchet and fell back.

The other Barbarian tried to strike her from behind but she ducked. Brit pole-axed him in the middle of his forehead. He dropped like a sack of shit and didn't get back up.

The Archer dipped an arrow in fire and sent it screaming at Brit, but Mikayla blocked with her shield and slashed the bow in two with her sword. The Archer looked down at the useless pieces of bow in his hand as Mikayla's left hook squashed in his nose.

The Sellsword had found his way back to his feet, but he stood unsteadily. "Don't be a coward," the Mongrel leader shouted. "They're only children."

The last Mongrel looked from his leader to the girls and back again. With a small cry of fear, he fled from the village Oppold.

"Useless nitwits," the scarred Berserker scowled. "Come on then, I'll take you all on."

"You leave them alone!"

They turned, and saw in the door of the inn, the innkeeper. His face was red with anger. "They've got your hooligans beat. Get out of here before they really show you what's what!"

Another villager stuck her head out the door of one of the few cottages not on fire. "Go back to Pyxis!" she shouted. "We haven't done anything to you people! Stay on your side of the river!"

The Berserker took a menacing step towards the villagers. Ib picked a stone and hurled it with all of his might at the scarred man, who deflected it with his axe-blade. He snarled at the child but was met with a volley of rocks from the rest of the villagers. Most clattered harmlessly off his armor but one struck him clear on the head.

The girls laughed as he raised his arms to defend

himself from the barrage. Deciding the odds were no longer in his favor, the Berserker shouted to his men, "Mongrels make tracks!"

The other Mongrels picked themselves up again, groaning. They scrambled for the edge of the village, vaulting over the low fence that encircled Oppold.

Before he left, the Berserker called, "I'll see you again, girlies. Don't think I'm through with you."

"Wait!" Brit yelled after him. "We need to kill you for experience!"

The scarred man quivered with rage but didn't say anything else.

"Did you see me?" Brit said. "I totally handed that Berserker his ass!"

Mikayla laughed. "That was awesome! Who do we fight next?"

The nearest cottage burned through, collapsing into pixels.

"Flames," Suzanne muttered. "We'll get some XP if we help save the village."

Half of Oppold was still on fire. The girls helped where they could. Some of the cottages were beyond saving. Brit collapsed these to prevent the flames from spreading. Mikayla and Suzanne joined in with the villagers bringing buckets of water from the well. It was hard work, made more difficult by the panicking villagers, but eventually the fires were extinguished. And even thought it wasn't real, Suzanne felt an odd mixture of pride when the last flames were put out.

Only two cottages and the inn remained standing.

"We should have finished the Mongrels," Brit complained. "Then we could've split."

The sound of staggered steps announced the arrival of the innkeeper, Hawthorne. "That you should have," he said, leaning on his stick more than ever. "But you three have already done enough for us."

"We'll help you rebuild," Mikayla said. Brit pantomimed gagging.

"Wouldn't do no good," Hawthorne replied. "No, I think it's time for us to make tracks for the Capital and throw ourselves on the king's mercy."

He sounded so disgusted by the prospect that at first Suzanne thought he was joking. But the other villagers were gathering what meager, unburned possessions they had and congregating in the town square.

"How far is it to the Capital?" Brit asked.

"Few days walk," the innkeeper said. "Just follow the Grand Highway and we'll get there soon enough."

"But what about monsters?" Mikayla asked. "What if the bandits catch up to you on the way there?"

"Then the bandits catch up to us on the way there."

Suzanne had never seen a more resigned face than that of Hawthorne the innkeeper. Suddenly, an idea came to her.

"Would you give us a moment?" she asked. The innkeeper shrugged and hobbled over to the rest of the villagers, where his grandchildren embraced him and helped him sit down.

"No," Brit said, before Suzanne even spoke.

"You don't know what I'm thinking," Suzanne replied.

"I do. You want us to take them all the way to

the Capital. There's no fucking way the first quest I accept is an escort mission."

"Come on!" Suzanne said. "I need to study the NPCs! What better way is there to do that than spending a bunch of time with them?"

"I would literally prefer anything else," Brit said. "You name it. I'll fight monsters, shit, I'll even learn how to craft items. As your friend, I'm begging you. Please don't make me do an escort mission."

"I'm already calling friend privileges," Suzanne replied.

Both of them turned to Mikayla. She shrugged. "Let's do it."

"You traitor," Brit muttered venomously. "Fine. But we don't go for free."

She strode confidently over to the inn, returning minutes later with a look of smug satisfaction on her face.

"We've been hired," she said. "If we get them all the way to Zenith City, they'll give us our five hundred gold back."

Chapter 7

"Why can't this be one of those games where you just warp between towns?" Brit asked.

"I'll add it to the next patch," Suzanne promised. She flipped through her Menu. To the NPCs it must have looked like she was waving her hands in the air, but Suzanne was double-checking her Quest Log.

ESCORTING OPPOLD appeared at the top of her Log. Good to know that the Log updated automatically.

"I'm not playing again until you update," Brit swore as Suzanne closed out of her Menu.

"Oh shut up," Mikayla said. "Try enjoying yourself for a change."

Brit groaned louder. Suzanne supposed she could understand Brit's frustration. They'd been walking for hours, after all. The traveling exhilarated Suzanne. The sense of distance covered reminded her of the road trips of her childhood, when she'd follow her parents into the family's sedan and her dad would just drive. She remembered watching the yellow lines disappear beneath the hood of the car while the engine purred contentment, the landscape a montage at such high speeds. And true, they were walking, not riding, and her companions were the villagers of Oppold and not her parents, but none of that stopped her from smiling and exulting in the crisp air of the Grand Highway.

And sure, Brit was complaining. But Brit complaining meant that she was in a good mood. She was walking beside Suzanne, taking a break from entertaining the children of Oppold, who regarded her as a hero.

"Brit!" Ib shouted, running up beside her. "You never finished the story! What happened to Retchen?" Suzanne flashed Brit a quick look—they had to be careful what they said to NPCs. They couldn't use words like *game* when describing Io within their earshot or the NPCs might get suspicious, but Brit had already lifted the little boy onto her shoulders and started running back towards the rest of the children. Suzanne decided she would walk back and see if she could pick up any information from what the kids said.

She arrived to hear the end of a story Brit was telling.

"After that," Brit said, "I freed all the slaves from the evil Queen Retchen's mines, and they all went happily back to their families."

Suzanne laughed, and Brit smiled. Of course, Brit would be making up stories; she'd know not to mention the real world. The children were hanging onto Brit's every word. Some, like Ib, were simply hanging onto her.

Suzanne was content just to watch. It was one thing working on the game alone, the hours spent poring over code, wondering what kind of characters it would generate. But watching Brit play with the children, watching the children themselves, who were as varied as any cluster of kids in the real world, was a different thing entirely. It was Suzanne's world working.

Even the parents of Oppold were distinct. They could be delighted that their children were playing, despite the circumstances, or concerned that their kids would be too exhausted to walk for the rest of the day. Some villagers were excited by the metropolis that was their destination, and others were wary of the city and the three strange girls who were accompanying them there. And some of the NPCs, like Hawthorne, who was now hobbling towards Suzanne, cared for each other, and loved each other just like people in the real world.

"How's it going?" she asked, holding out an arm for him to support himself.

"Good," he rasped, but the strain of travel was evident on his face. Hawthorne looked like the last NPC who should be making the multi-day journey to Zenith City. Suzanne couldn't help but admire his resolve, even if it was as a result of an algorithm. Despite its name, the Grand Highway was just a dirt road.

"It's good to see them kids laughing again. Haven't been much cause for it since the first raids."

"When did they start?" Suzanne asked.

"Two years back, I think. No warning or nothing like that. Just a bunch of hooligans from Pyxis showing up and grabbing whatever was valuable."

"They're from Pyxis?" Suzanne asked.

Hawthorne gave her a quizzical look.

"Yes, Pyxis. You know, that kingdom all of Altair is at war with?"

Suzanne blushed. She would have to be careful with her reactions. The war with Pyxis was news to her—she had never programmed anything like that into Io. Still, it seemed only natural that the NPCs might end up fighting each other. And she supposed it was kind of cool that, even as its creator, Io could surprise her. She just hoped the surprises weren't too unpleasant.

Hawthorne was still staring at her, expecting some kind of justification. "Our village was . . . very isolated," she said lamely.

Apparently, it was enough for Hawthorne. "Well,

these raids are what started the war. Pyxians showing up all over the countryside. Apparently, they're looting for Energite crystals. Fat lot of good it'll do them, as we had about as many crystals as we have help from the king."

"Watch what you say, Hawthorne," one of the villagers called from nearby.

"And why should I?" the former innkeeper replied. "What kind of king lets his people suffer while he holes up in his castle in the sky?"

"The king's done great things!" the other villager retorted.

Hawthorne shook his stick in anger. "You name two things that Ramses has done since his coronation that have helped us common folk and I'll hop the rest of the way to Zenith City on one foot."

The other NPCs fell silent. Suzanne's mind raced to assimilate the new information. First a war and now a crystal shortage? Well, that was easily addressable by adjusting the frequency of crystals in loot drops.

She glanced up at her Energite reserve. It was

still full as she hadn't used any special attacks since starting this play through. But she'd have to tell Brit and Mikayla to be careful. Not only was there no guarantee of replenishing their reservoirs, but using special attacks when there was a shortage of Energite would be sure to draw attention to them. They should try to blend in with the Citizens so Suzanne could see the AI behaving normally. Flex too much muscle and they'd get a reputation that would warp all their interactions.

The silence was broken by loud giggles as Brit, with children still hanging onto her, came careening past. A sad smile broke out on Hawthorne's face as he watched them pass.

"They used to do that with their dad. He was a Fighter," Hawthorne said quietly.

"Went in the first raid. My only son. His wife, too, and the rest in the village who had classes. The Pyxians rounded them up and . . . "

The pain in his voice sounded so real to Suzanne. "I'm sorry," she said. "I lost my mother when I was young, too."

The words were out before Suzanne realized what she was saying.

Suzanne turned away. The last place Suzanne wanted to get pity from was an NPC.

Luckily, Mikayla returned from scouting before Hawthorne could say anything else. She was a Ranger, a balanced class in combat but with a handful of useful other abilities. Rangers could see farther and hear better than other classes, which made them excellent scouts and trackers. They lacked the brute strength of Fighters or Barbarians but more than made up for it with the diverse range of weapons they could use.

"There's a grove up ahead that would make a good place to rest," she reported. "The trees look pretty thick, so we'd be safe from a big attack. We should be able to reach it by nightfall."

"Did you see any monsters?" Suzanne asked. So far, the Grand Highway had been monster-free. Maybe that would be true for daylight hours, but there were bound to be monsters at night. The highway wasn't a town and so nothing, besides the density of NPCs, stopped monsters from wandering on to it. Besides Brit, Mikayla, and Suzanne, no one in their group could really fight. Citizens might be capable merchants, smiths, and innkeepers, but they were terrible in a fight.

"It looked empty," Mikayla said. "But we'll have to take turns at watch."

Suzanne called over Brit, who managed to free herself from the children. After Suzanne shared what she had learned from Hawthorne with both Brit and Mikayla, they agreed that the best course of action would be to hole up in the grove for the night.

"Do we have enough time to play another day?" Mikayla asked.

That confused Suzanne until she realized Mikayla meant real-world time. She motioned Mikayla close and dropped her voice so Hawthorne couldn't hear.

"I think so. The NPCs' levels are so low that nothing too scary will find us, but we could be in for a night of farming."

By farming, she meant farming for XP, or killing low-level monsters. In most games, this was a monotonous task, but Suzanne realized that in Io, they'd have to spend the night actually killing every creature that attacked. She was excited to see what the game would throw at them.

By the time the grove came into view, the sun was sinking in the sky. The villagers knew that monsters were more active at night. Some of them kept glancing from the grove to the sun, unsure if they'd make it there in time. Some, like the villager who had argued with Hawthorne earlier, loudly expressed their disapproval of the plan. But most were content to push forward to the grove.

They reached it before sundown. Through the dense trees, Suzanne watched the technicolor setting of the sun. But there was little time for rest. Soon it would be dark and things would be bumping in the night.

Chapter 8

During her watch, Suzanne saw a few goblins and some gargantulas—spiders the size of bears—creeping through the trees. She was so curious about the monsters that she almost forgot to fight them. When Suzanne's shift was over and Mikayla came to relieve her, Suzanne was fighting off the small horde that had assembled while she was busy ogling a gargantula's fangs.

She went back to the campsite and passed out. After what felt like seconds, Brit woke her and they shepherded the villagers back on the road, marching north. As opposed to the day before, they no longer had the road to themselves.

From the east and west, caravans of merchants, bands of mercenaries, and what looked like entire villages of people joined onto the Grand Highway. As the Highway filled with more NPCs, it also became better paved and wider. No longer just a mound of packed earth, it was now complete with roadside inns every few miles and even lanes dividing the travelers by speed. The villagers of Oppold soon found themselves crowded into something resembling a marching formation, just to avoid getting run over by the horse-drawn carts of merchants.

Suzanne watched the horses. She hadn't added them to the game independent of carts yet, so they were a kind of item. But maybe she could reprogram them as monsters and make certain kinds of monsters tamable. That would open up a whole realm of possibility. She shivered at just the thought of it.

Mikayla was staring at the other NPCs with interest.

"I think they're refugees," she said, pointing to a particularly ashen-faced group of Citizens. "You think it was the Mongrels?"

Brit shrugged. "Either the Mongrels or some other dickheads. Real nice world you made here, Suze."

A look of indignation appeared on Suzanne's face. "Don't blame me. I only made the monsters."

The number of refugees troubled Suzanne. It was one thing for part of the kingdom to be under attack, but for this many villagers to be displaced there would have to be serious problems in Altair. Or maybe her NPC generator was way off.

"Maybe this Ramses guy is a shitty king," she muttered. That was the third option.

Brit laughed at that, but she wasn't the only one who heard. A group of NPCs was walking nearby. As the Grand Highway became more crowded, other classed NPCs had arrived. As opposed to the Citizens, classed NPCs could fight. They were like the Mongrels but their character icons were a neutral gray instead of red.

Some of the classed NPCs were on escort quests, like the girls, but most were mercenaries. The band closest to them appeared to be a trio for hire. One of them, a fellow with drooping eyelids and what looked like a small guitar slung over his shoulder, chuckled when Suzanne insulted the king.

"Don't be saying that too loud," he warned. "Especially once we get to the Capital."

"Do you know how long it'll be?" Mikayla asked.

The musician shrugged. "Any thoughts, Samara?" he asked his companion standing next to him.

"Should be by tomorrow afternoon," she called back. She was much shorter than the musician, but built more solidly. She wore a longbow strapped to her back that was as tall as she was. At her hip was a quiver of barbed arrows. Their third companion looked like a Fighter, but instead of any weapons he carried two shields.

"Well, there's your answer," the musician replied. Suzanne noticed a slight lilt in his voice as he spoke. "My name's Picciotto. And you are?"

"Suzanne," she answered. "And that's Brit, and that's Mikayla. We're escorting some villagers to the Capital."

"Aren't we all?" Picciotto grandly replied.

"No," Samara answered pointedly. "We aren't. We're going to find work to support your lazy bones."

If the barb bothered Picciotto, he didn't show it. Wheeling around, he began to sing:

Oh Samara! So kindly! So beauteous and fair!
Her eyes the same color as her mustache hair!

He would have kept singing were it not for Samara pulling an arrow from her quiver and pointing it towards him.

"I know I'm supposed to shoot these," she said. "But you probably don't want me stabbing you with one."

"Oh no," Picciotto replied, feigning horror. "I know all too well what you're capable of."

The girls all laughed at their play fighting. Picciotto and Samara's third companion merely nodded, acknowledging the tomfoolery.

"What's the matter, Desmond?" Picciotto asked. "Have you been charmed senseless by the breathtaking Brit, the sensational Suzanne, and the mysterious Mikayla?"

"No," the massive Desmond replied. And for the rest of the walk, he didn't say anything else.

But nothing would keep Picciotto silent. For the rest of their march he regaled them with tales of his various deeds, Samara jumping in to correct his wildest exaggerations.

They were indeed heading to the Capital to look for work, Suzanne learned. They had been traveling around the South for the duration of the war, but with the recent upticks in raids from Pyxians and the mass migration from villages towards the cities, they were finding it increasingly hard to secure paying work out in the boonies. "I mean, don't get me wrong," Picciotto said, gesticulating enthusiastically. "It's fine looking after Citizens pro bono, it's just that these strings are expensive, and, well, we've a more specialized skill set than most mercenaries."

Suzanne understood, but Brit and Mikayla seemed lost. Picciotto was all too happy to enlighten them.

"Take Samara, for example. Best shot in the

East, but not so great up close and personal. And Desmond doesn't even carry weapons!"

Suzanne saw Desmond roll his eyes. Picciotto didn't have any weapons either, she realized.

"Yeah, why is that?" Mikayla asked.

"He's a Guardian," Samara explained, knocking on his breast plate. "Built to take hits." Guardians were an advanced class, a variant of Fighters that maximized defense instead of offense. But still possessing a Fighter's strength, they could use their shields with crushing effectiveness at short range. Suzanne smiled to herself. She'd come up with the idea for Guardians while reading her dad's old comic books. But Desmond looked nothing like the Guardian from DC Comics. His shields were the size of van doors. He was as big as Brit was, a mountain of armor.

Brit looked over Desmond. Suzanne could tell she was weighing the merits of being a Guardian. But Suzanne knew that Brit would never pick such a defensive role; when it was time for the girls to transition to advanced classes, she'd probably choose to be a Berserker or some other class with staggering offensive capabilities.

"Okay," Brit said, "but what can you do, music man?"

"Absolutely nothing," Picciotto replied, winking. "I'm a burden to my friends and generally a waste of space."

"Truer words have never been spoken," Samara agreed.

The joking continued until Ib showed up, on behalf of Hawthorne. The villagers of Oppold were growing weary from traveling and wanted to know how much longer it would take them to reach the Capital. The girls followed Ib back to his grandfather and the rest of the villagers, where they relayed what Samara had said.

"Good to hear," Hawthorne said. "I don't know how much further these old feet would carry me."

"Well I could always give you a lift," Brit said.

Hawthorne puffed out his chest. "We're a far sight from that."

For the rest of the day, Suzanne contented herself

to watch the crowds on the Grand Highway. Soon, on the horizon, there appeared a cloud, floating low over what looked like four pillars. But as they continued down the Highway, Suzanne realized that the cloud hadn't moved or changed size. Was there a glitch in the weather program for the game? Then she realized what she was looking at. She almost thought about pointing it out to Mikayla and Brit, but she didn't want to ruin the surprise.

"It's a city," Mikayla said. She too had been staring at the cloud, but with a Ranger's vision. "That cloud is a city! Those pillars must hold it up."

Suzanne laughed. "Why do you think it's called Zenith City?"

Soon Suzanne and Brit could also make out the spires and structures of the city on the pillars. Below the city, clustered around each of the four pillars were more buildings, suburbs to the Capital.

"Those buildings—they're huge," Brit raved. "I mean, if I can see them from all the way over here, then they must be as big as stadiums, easily!"

"I take it you three have never seen Zenith City before," Picciotto said. "Quite a sight, no?"

A huge smile spread across Suzanne's face. She could hardly wait for their next session so she could see what her crowning achievement was really like.

Chapter 9

High school is known for its sucky days. Even graded on that curve, Thursday was a real shit show.

It started before school even began. Suzanne was up early working on the latest patch to her game when her dad knocked on her door. He had just come back from his shift at the campus security center and was still wearing his blue guard's uniform.

"Sweetie?" His voice was muffled through the door.

Suzanne saved her code. She double-checked that the TII helmets were hidden away and opened it, letting him in.

"I'm actually granted entrance," he said, pretending to be in awe.

Suzanne gave him a half-hearted laugh.

He grimaced. "Just wanted to remind you that I'm still going to New Jersey this weekend to see Mike."

Suzanne remembered, despite having done her best to forget. The specter of them moving had hovered over her head all week, making it hard for her to concentrate, whether she was in class or Io.

"Will you be okay here by yourself? I can always get Mrs. Baron to look after you."

Suzanne shuddered. Mrs. Baron was the old lady who lived across the hall with an indeterminate number of cats. Indeterminate because she neither neutered her cats nor fed them. Suzanne wasn't sure if she had ever seen the same cat twice.

"I'll be fine," she said.

Her dad gave her a look. "And you promise you'll go outside? And remember to eat? I don't want to come back from Jersey and find that you've died from malnutrition."

Suzanne rolled her eyes. "I can take care of myself."

He didn't question her further, but he also didn't leave. She saw he was staring at the digital photo frame on her desktop. Standing up, she tiptoed around the piles of dirty clothes and gave him a hug.

"I know you'll nail the interview," she said. "I love you, okay? But now I've got to get ready for school."

Her dad patted her stiffly on the head and walked out, closing the door behind him.

Suzanne exhaled. Despite what she had said, part of her was hoping her dad would screw up majorly. If he didn't get the job then they wouldn't have to think about moving. But another part of her knew that her dad was embarrassed to be a security guard. He used to teach on the campus, but he had been such a wreck after her mom died that now all he did was guard empty buildings. Suzanne wondered if he resented that, resented the fact that an old department buddy gave him the job out of pity. She wanted to tell him she understood why he wanted a new job and a new start.

But why couldn't he find another job closer to where they were? Even if they moved to another part of Maryland she could still see Brit and Mikayla on the weekends.

Suzanne didn't drive. New Jersey might as well be on another planet.

In homeroom, Mikayla looked as crappy as Suzanne felt.

"Coach made me stay late," she said. She was slumped over her desk. "Said I had to fold towels until I learned the value of teamwork."

Mikayla sat up straight and looked Suzanne right in the eye. "If I have to fetch Gretchen another fucking towel I'll go crazy. It's that simple. I'll just go nuts."

Well, Suzanne mused, *I guess misery does love company*.

Suspiciously, Brit was absent. Mikayla said she had given Brit a ride to school, but Brit had gone to the bathroom instead of homeroom and had never shown up.

Suzanne didn't see Brit until history class. Mr. Olson gave them a group project, so immediately Brit slid her desk toward Suzanne's.

"Where were you in homeroom?" Suzanne whispered.

"Operation Fuck Gretchen," Brit whispered back.

"Oh no," Suzanne said. "What did you do?"

But Brit wouldn't say. Suzanne kept prodding her while she filled in the dates of the ratification of amendments to the Constitution, while Brit kept evading her questions.

"If you don't tell me, I'm not going to finish," Suzanne said.

"Yeah, right. Like you wouldn't do an assignment."

"I'm serious," Suzanne whispered. She was, in fact, bluffing, but it irritated her that Brit didn't even consider the threat.

"Nah," Brit said. "Besides, I don't want to ruin the surprise."

The PA system in the room crackled. The voice

of the school secretary came through the speaker loud and clear. "Brittany Acosta, please come to the principal's office."

✦

Instead of going to lunch after the bell rang, Suzanne headed to the main office. She wasn't surprised to see Mikayla sitting there as well. Brit must have texted on her way to receive sentencing. Whatever Operation Fuck Gretchen was, Suzanne hoped it was worth it.

Lunch was nearly over when Brit emerged. Gretchen strode out of the office with a triumphant smirk right after her. She paused to give Mikayla and Suzanne a nasty glare before strutting off down the hallway, her heels clicking on the linoleum.

When Brit went to the bathroom during homeroom, she went to the one in the girls' locker room. There was guaranteed to be no one else in there as everybody had to be in homeroom.

Among other things, Brit happened to know the master combination for all the lockers in school. It was a handy code to know. Half the student body owed Brit for unlocking their lockers after they forgot the combination. But the master code was useful for slightly less upstanding purposes as well.

First, she opened up Gretchen's gym locker. It was easy to find, as it stank of perfume and was filled to bursting with cosmetics. After clearing a space, Brit balanced three two-liters of Diet Coke in the locker. Brit never paid attention in science class, but every kid knew what happened when you combined Diet Coke and Mentos. Brit slammed Gretchen's locker shut as foam erupted out of the bottles.

Gretchen had stopped by her locker during second period only to find everything inside covered in a layer of sticky crud. Her cheer outfit looked like it had been used to clean up the cafeteria floor. Literally screeching from rage, she had stalked up and down the rows of lockers, interrogating everyone in the vicinity.

Brit's prank was almost perfect. Almost. She didn't

realize the foam would erupt into other lockers, damaging their contents as well. And although there were no security cameras in the locker rooms, there were plenty cameras leading into the gym. Brit was the only student who entered the locker room during homeroom. Add that to her long history of misbehavior and the administration had enough circumstantial evidence to give her a month of detention.

But that wasn't enough for Gretchen. Her laptop, her car keys, and plenty of other "irreplaceable" belongings were damaged beyond repair. Her parents threatened the school with legal action unless a more severe punishment was administered. Considering their active role in the PTA and skittish around mentions of a lawsuit, the school upped Brit's punishment to a month of detention and thirty hours of community service, to be fulfilled by picking up trash.

"Look on the bright side," Mikayla said. "Now we both have to pick up after her royal pain in the ass."

Brit flipped Mikayla the bird. "Thank god we have

the TII," Brit said. "I don't know what I'd do if I was forced to spend all my time in this shitty reality."

When Suzanne didn't reply, Brit gave her a concerned look. "We can still go to Io, right? You didn't lose the helmets or anything?"

"No," Suzanne said. Reluctantly she explained what was going on with her dad. How they might be moving out of state. By the time she was done, Brit's frustration had turned into mortification.

"When's the interview?" Mikayla asked.

"This weekend."

"Are you kidding?" Brit said. "You could be gone like next month!"

Suzanne's stomach sank. She hadn't thought it would happen that fast, but how could she know?

"Okay," Mikayla said, after they had wallowed in collective misery for a minute. "Okay here's what we do. Your dad leaves on Friday, right? Well, that gives us three days to beat Io. Clear the baddest boss, max out our characters, and purge evil from the land or something."

"Yeah, but you've got a basketball game Saturday

night," Suzanne said. She never went to Perry Hall High's games herself, but hanging out with Mikayla had taught her the schedule.

"Whatever. This is more important."

Brit laughed. "Finally we find something more important than cheerleading."

Mikayla gave her a fierce look. "We don't have time to feel sorry for ourselves. We've got to make the time we have count."

"Aye aye, captain," Brit said saluting. It pained Suzanne to think that soon she would have to leave. She wouldn't be able to see Brit and Mikayla clowning around again.

She turned her head to the side to hide her expression from them. "My place right after school," she said. "Bring some snacks, bring your pjs. We're going to speed run this bitch."

Chapter 10

Suzanne rolled into school on Friday excited. She had spent all of Thursday night working on the latest patch to Io. Some of the monsters had been scaled up in toughness, but those were minor changes. Brit kept texting her to make the game "epic," and she wasn't shy on her suggestions. Number one on her list was permanent death.

When you died in most games you simply rebooted your save file and re-spawned where you had last saved the game. But Brit's suggestion was a hallmark of more hardcore gaming experiences. In some games, a dead character was a dead character.

No 2nd chances, Brit texted Suzanne. All or nuthin.

The more Suzanne turned over the idea in her head, the more she liked it. If this was going to be their best shot at clearing Io then why not make it a real challenge? Besides, Suzanne didn't envision herself dying in Io. She barely considered the possibility. She didn't know if her pride could handle her losing at her own game.

The weather on Friday was gray and stormy in direct contrast to Suzanne's mood. She was beaming sunshine, even though the school bus was late and she got soaked waiting for it to arrive. What did it matter when she had the prospect of a weekend in Io to look forward to?

Her mood held through a math test and an English presentation. The cafeteria served leftovers but even that couldn't put a damper on her mood. Suzanne was beginning to think that nothing could ruin her day.

And then she walked into Mr. Wells's class for Intro to Tech.

"What a psycho!" Gretchen was loudly exclaiming.

"I can't believe they let her back in this school. I mean, imagine if I had been there."

She paused for dramatic effect. Suzanne walked straight to her seat. She tried to ignore Gretchen but as always that was easier said than done.

"She could have hurt me. I mean really hurt me."

"I'll hurt you," Suzanne muttered under her breath.

Apparently Gretchen had heard. "What was that, Suzandroid? Trying to join your psycho friend in community service?"

"You know what, Gretchen?" Suzanne said, standing up. She saw Mikayla shake her head and mouth the word, *No*. But Suzanne wasn't going to stand for Gretchen's shit, not today. She stomped across the room and smacked Gretchen right in the face.

There was a stunned silence in the room.

Gretchen gingerly placed a hand on her cheek. Suzanne's insides were squirming. What had she done? Now Gretchen was going to wreck her life, too.

Then Suzanne remembered that her life was about to be wrecked anyway. Suddenly, the rainy clouds seemed far more appropriate.

"A month's detention? You?" Brit's skepticism arched her eyebrows. They were walking across the parking lot to Mikayla's car.

"Yeah," Suzanne said. She could hardly believe it herself. It had also been hard for Principal Higgins to believe. "Of all my students," she said to Suzanne, "I least expected this from you."

Then she dropped her voice to a confidential tone. "Your father informed us that you might be moving soon. If you behave yourself in detention we don't have to put this on your permanent record."

"Like I give a shit," Suzanne said. But she knew she was just talking tough. Deep down, the thought of a month's detention on her personal record gave her chills.

"Still. I'd do two months if I could have been the one to smack her."

"Don't say that," Mikayla said, unlocking her car. "The shit she was saying . . . just be thankful you weren't there. She's looking for any excuse to mess with us now."

Suzanne moved towards the back seat, but to her surprise, Brit had ceded shotgun.

"No, no," she said, waving her hands when Suzanne motioned for her to go up front. "You punch Gretchen, you get shotgun."

"She only slapped her." Mikayla was trying to sound cross but she couldn't stop smiling.

They pulled up to Suzanne's apartment. Suzanne unlocked the door. "Dad?" she called. No response. He had left before she got up that morning, leaving only a note covered in *X*'s and *O*'s. Suzanne crumpled it into her pocket before Brit saw it and teased her for it.

Suzanne began to explain the features she had added to the TII since their last session, but Brit waved her off.

"Speed run! No time for notes! Speed run!"

Suzanne tried to argue, but Brit and Mikayla began chanting, "Speed run!" over and over.

"Okay," Suzanne said, "then let's get this show on the road."

✦

They had last stopped at a roadside inn with Zenith City on the horizon. That's where they reappeared when they logged back in. Outside the inn they passed a large sign that read: FOUR PILLARS AHEAD. But it was hardly necessary. By the time they reached the sign, the sun had passed behind Zenith City. And so they approached the metropolis already in its shadow.

That penumbral suburb, the Southern Pillar, was cast entirely in eerie twilight. Suburbanites scurried about in permanent dusk, their way only partially lit by the flickering flames of lamplight. The merchant carts that had followed the refugee train split off, heading for their respective shops and homes. Uneasy murmurs broke out among the refugees.

But Suzanne was beyond excited. They had finally

made it to the Capital! Brit and Mikayla shared her excitement. They were going to meet the king and get a quest a hundred times cooler than any escort mission.

The suburb itself was beautiful, if not slightly worn. The Grand Highway lead directly into the main boulevard of the Southern Pillar. Variegated townhouses lined both sides of the road. A far cry from the cottages of Oppold, the townhouses were multiple stories tall, made of a smooth yet lustrous stone. But as tall as the houses were, the Southern Pillar, rising from the center of the suburb to the base of Zenith City, dwarfed everything else.

The sights captivated the refugees. Suzanne guessed that most of them had never seen the Capital, only heard of it in the tales of merchants and other travelers. That was good—their wide-eyed awe disguised her own ignorance and gave her every excuse to gawk openly. Peering down side streets, she saw all manner of shops and taverns and ornately decorated buildings that must have been guildhalls.

Suzanne noticed that while the refugees stared at

the sights and Civilians around them, the suburban-ites barely noticed them. They would look up briefly, acknowledging the crowd of new arrivals, before continuing on their own business.

Nudging Brit, Suzanne said, "I guess they're used to crowds of refugees."

The suburb was much larger than it looked. It took them more than an hour after entering Zenith City's shadow to make their way to the base of the Southern Pillar, their progress slowed by the rubber-necking refugees and the narrow roads of the suburb.

When they reached the pillar, the refugees milled about, uncertain where to go next. They had been forced into something of a marching formation while passing through the narrow suburban streets, but now they spread out in the pillar square. Some, tired after the long journey, sat down on the ground and rested. Others continued to take in the new sights with nervous eyes.

Suzanne motioned to the other girls, and they began to walk around the pillar, inspecting it. The pillar was as wide around as the village of Oppold had been, a perfect cylinder. At four points along the base was the same insignia: a crimson orb resting atop a four-pillared podium. The insignias glowed. Suzanne realized that they were some kind of gemstones, embedded in the pillar.

Mikayla was the first to hear the sound.

"Something's moving inside the pillar," she said.

And soon enough the others could hear it as well: a groaning noise, like machinery straining.

"It's falling apart!" an NPC shouted.

"We're all going to be crushed!" cried another.

"Oh, for fuck's sake," Brit muttered.

The sound grew louder and the panic spread throughout the NPCs. They backed away from the pillar. Some fled back down the road they had arrived on. But Suzanne saw the suburbanites continuing along their business, some looking amused at the panic of the refugees.

"I think something's traveling down it." Mikayla held a hand to the pillar. "It's vibrating," she said. "We should probably back up."

They joined the NPCs a safe distance away from

the pillar, standing near Hawthorne and his grand-children. Brit immediately set about distracting Ib, who had begun to cry. Suzanne asked Hawthorne if he knew what was happening, but he was as mystified as they were. The mechanical sound was deafening now, and more refugees were running in panic.

But then the four insignias flashed bright red. Then they swung open on panels, to reveal a compartment within the pillar, completely filled with soldiers.

There were Fighters and Rangers, and other initial classes like Archers, Sellswords, and Knights. But predominately, the soldiers were in advanced classes. Paladins with their long swords stood shoulder to shoulder with axe-bearing Berserkers. A group of Snipers exited with their bows already drawn. Suzanne saw Guardians with their massive shields, and, towering above the rest, lance wielding Dragoons. Each wore armor bearing the same insignia as was inscribed on the pillar.

Hawthorne gathered Ib and Henny close to himself. Suzanne instinctively reached for her daggers and both Mikayla and Brit readied their own weapons.

But the soldiers simply filed out of the compartment and arranged themselves in formation. They waited with perfect discipline as a small, squat man, made his way out into the square.

The bald man wore a long, gray cloak that covered all of his limbs. He moved gracefully, so that his cloak seemed more mist than fabric. Even in the shadow of Zenith City, Suzanne could see red gems gleaming on the end of long chains that dangled from his ears.

In a voice like gravel, he spoke loud to the assembled refugees.

"Citizens and subjects of Altair, on behalf of his majesty, King Ramses, I welcome you to the Southern Pillar. My name is Burgrave and I am an official in his majesty's court."

He paused and instantly murmurs broke out among the crowd. Suzanne stared at the short official; despite his stature, he was clearly in command of the assembled forces. His age was hard to guess. His face was worn, but not lined like Hawthorne's. And his expression remained completely neutral as he waited patiently for the refugees to quiet down.

"I understand your journey here has been difficult. His majesty has provided temporary quarters, so you may rest until more permanent accommodations can be arranged. Wollman?"

A Paladin with a saber and a rondel thrust through his belt stepped forward out of the assembled soldiers. He wore a red cape over his armor and his face was covered by his helm.

"Wollman will lead those in need of rest or those seeking refuge to the Eastern Pillar."

"Follow me," Wollman said, immediately setting off east. More than half the crowd set off after him.

"I guess this is goodbye, then," Hawthorne said. "Five hundred gold, as promised." He handed the gold to Brit who put it in her inventory. With a final smile of gratitude, he set off with his grandchildren and the rest of the refugees.

"We should have let them keep the gold," Mikayla said.

"Fat chance," Brit replied.

The remaining travelers were the mercenaries and other classed NPCs who had joined in the train. In the face of the soldiers, the travelers looked completely inexperienced. Most, Suzanne realized, were not fully equipped with armor. Some didn't even have weapons.

Suzanne saw Picciotto whispering something to Desmond. The Guardian let out a single gruff chuckle. Samara saw Suzanne and waved, smiling. Suzanne waved back.

Burgrave cleared his throat and everyone, including Picciotto, fell silent.

"I assume those remaining wish to volunteer for his majesty's royal forces. Those interested in enlistment shall form a line by Captain Crux. You will be examined to ensure that your loyalties are to his highness and the kingdom only."

As Burgrave spoke, the most massive of the Dragoons stepped forward. In the real world, he would have been over eight feet tall. Yet for all his massiveness, when he removed his helm, he had a kind face. The Dragoon, Crux, set his maul down and stepped off to the side.

Some of the travelers moved towards the gigantic Dragoon, while others held back. Clearly Burgrave's speech had unsettled some of them. Suzanne wondered what he meant by examination.

Burgrave spoke again. "No fears, fellow Citizens. If you are true subjects of Altair, then you have nothing to fear."

"And if we aren't?" called a voice from among those who had held back.

"Then you have something to fear," the official blandly replied.

A line formed in front of Crux. As each NPC stepped forward, Burgrave stared intensely at them before waving them along. The other reluctant NPCs, after seeing how harmless the test was, joined the line.

The line moved quickly, but not quick enough for Brit's taste.

"This is supposed to be a speed run," she muttered.

"Calm down," Suzanne told her. "We need to wait until the end so we get a sweet quest." She'd written in that bit of code last night and would have told Brit and Mikayla about it if they hadn't been in such a rush to get in the game.

When the last NPC, a blond Lancer, received his okay, the bald official turned towards the girls.

"If you'd please," he said, beckoning them forward.

Before Suzanne or Brit could react, Mikayla was marching straight towards Burgrave. As she crossed the distance between the girls and the soldiers, passing Crux's maul, two soldiers stepped forwards and drew their swords.

Mikayla blinked, but didn't flinch. "Hi," she said. "My name's Mikayla."

"Hello, Citizen," the robed man responded, amused.

"I'm not a Citizen of Altair," she replied.

It was as if an electric current had passed through the soldiers. They snapped to attention. Their weapons flashed and their bodies tensed for action. The NPCs who had cleared the checkpoint stood on tiptoes, trying to get a better view of the scene.

Suzanne almost couldn't look.

The diminutive official did not start as all the other soldiers did. "May I ask if you come from the kingdom of Pyxis?" As before, he kept his voice perfectly level.

"We're not from there either."

"We?" he asked.

Mikayla turned and motioned to Brit and Suzanne. Suzanne wondered if Mikayla knew what she was doing, but Brit was already dragging her forward. Soon all three girls stood within range of Zenith City's Royal Guard.

"We come from a faraway land," Suzanne said. Immediately she regretted how stupid those words sounded.

"We came to help out with your monster problems," Brit said.

"We seek an audience with King Ramses," Mikayla added.

The official looked from girl to girl as each of them spoke. Up close, Suzanne saw that his eyes were the same misty gray as the rest of his robe. He must be using a skill, Suzanne realized—that's how he can tell where the NPCs were from. But she hadn't programmed any ability like that into the game.

Finally, he spoke. "I see."

He pointed at Mikayla. "You say you are Mikayla? And who are your companions?"

Brit gave a small, uncertain bow. "I'm Brit."

"And I'm Suzanne."

"Brit and Suzanne," he repeated, "and Mikayla. Very well. You are all under arrest."

At his words, his escorts stepped forward. Mikayla's hand was on the hilt of her sword, and Suzanne already had a pair of daggers drawn. We can't possibly win a fight, Suzanne thought, but maybe we can get away.

Brit, meanwhile, had grabbed Crux's maul. Grunting from the strain, she lifted the massive maul and held it above Burgrave's bald head.

"You take another step," she said to the soldiers, "and short stuff here is going to need a new pumpkin."

The soldiers stopped, looking to Burgrave for instructions. As unfazed as ever, he waved his hand. The soldiers lowered their weapons, falling back.

"We don't want to hurt anyone," Suzanne said. "Please, we just want to speak with the king."

"Better make up your mind quick," Brit cut in. "It's getting pretty heavy."

"You leave those girls alone!"

The soldiers, the girls, and even Burgrave turned to see Hawthorne, leaning on his stick, standing at the eastern entrance to the square.

"They're heroes, they are. Saved my entire village and walked us all the way here."

"Are you referring to the village of Oppold?" Burgrave asked.

"That's the one. Of course, there ain't much there now, but they saved us all, they did."

Burgrave turned from Hawthorne back to the girls. "I had received news of some foreigners traveling with this refugee train, but we assumed it was Pyxians in disguise. I see that you are, as you say, from a faraway land."

Suzanne blushed.

But Burgrave smiled. "Please, come with me. And Brit, was it? You may leave the maul."

With a flick of his wrist, he smacked the hammer out of her hands. Brit wasn't ready and she stumbled, trying to regain her balance. The hammer fell to the ground with a loud boom, cracking another tile.

"I shall escort you to the king. I personally guarantee that as long as you do not draw weapons again within city limits, no harm shall come to you."

Turning to one of the soldiers, he said, "Take the volunteers to the barracks. I will escort these three to the palace."

"Sir," the soldier began, but Burgrave silenced him with a wave of his hand. "Do as I say. I assure you, I will be fine."

Casting suspicious looks at the girls, the soldiers marshaled the volunteers and set off towards the Western Pillar. Picciotto blew them a kiss as he passed. Samara simply looked worried.

When the soldiers were on their way, Burgrave beckoned the girls to follow him into the pillar. The doors closed behind them. Suzanne heard the same grinding noise as, with a jerk, the elevator ascended, taking the girls to meet the NPC who thought he was a king.

Chapter 11

While the elevator sped upwards, the grinding mechanical sound was reduced to a hum. It was mostly dark within the pillar, although light filtered down from above. As Suzanne's eyes adjusted to the darkness, she noticed that there were no buttons inside the compartment. Whatever was making the elevator rise was controlled from somewhere else.

"What did you mean earlier?" Burgrave asked Brit.

"By what?"

"When you said I would need a new pumpkin. I assumed you meant it as a threat but I was not sure what you were threatening."

"Oh," Brit said. "I guess I meant I'd hit you in the head or something."

"I see," he replied. "Mind, when you meet the king, you should be more respectful."

Mikayla nodded. "Of course."

Soon the elevator began to slow. Then it came to a stop. The platform rose up, and the girls found themselves in the middle of a beautiful plaza.

The sky above was a vibrant blue. The air was crisp and biting. NPCs strutted by, dressed to impress in furs and embroidered clothing. Many wore the four-pillared insignia of Altair, although their representations were far more stylized than the engravings on the soldiers' armor. Compared to the villagers of Oppold, the Zenith Citizens looked like NPCs from a different game.

And the buildings of Zenith City looked wildly different as well. They were far more extravagant than the houses in the suburbs and as they were not in constant shade, their bright colors shone brilliantly.

Suzanne was so dazzled by the opulence that she did not realize the girls were surrounded. Members of the City Guard lined the platform. Some of the passing Citizens stopped to gawk at the scene. Apparently, the City Guard assembling was a far more common sight in the suburbs.

Burgrave set off at such a pace that the girls were jogging to keep up. The City Guard split; most of them, including the guards with the girls' weapons, marched off, while some followed the girls and Burgrave at a distance.

The crowd of Citizens parted to allow Burgrave to pass. Some of the most finely dressed made gestures towards the official, but most simply averted their eyes and stepped aside. Suzanne walked faster and caught up to the short, bald man.

"How did you know we aren't from Altair?" she asked.

"Mikayla said so, did she not?"

"Yeah, but besides that. When you stared at us and double-checked."

Without slowing his pace, he replied, "Mikayla is a Ranger, correct? Then like her, I see."

"But there's no ability like that!" she protested.

Burgrave fixed her with a quizzical look. "May I ask how you are so certain?"

"Oh," she replied, scrambling for an excuse. "I spent a lot of time studying combat. I've just never heard of such an ability, is all I meant."

"As far as I know, I am the first to develop such a skill."

The implications of his words almost stopped Suzanne cold. How could an NPC develop a new skill? The game's AI could make new characters, but new abilities? How was that even possible?

But she knew that if she pressed Burgrave for answers, she'd only raise his suspicions further. After all, he had been able to tell where NPCs were from just by looking at them. What would he see when he looked at the girls?

Suzanne saw green player icons floating over Brit and Mikayla's heads and the same gray icons marking all the NPCs. Maybe Burgrave's ability let him see things like a player did? Either way, Suzanne knew she had to be careful when dealing with the little official.

They passed through more plazas, each as splendid as the others. There were huge fountains where children splashed in the waters and musicians played. A bazaar filled one plaza, where ornamental swords encrusted with precious stones were exchanged for towers of gold coins. Off in the distance, Suzanne could see a coliseum, bigger than any professional stadium she had ever seen. Listening carefully, she could make out the cheerful cries of the audience.

The city began to blend together. For the girls, who had spent the past days traveling through the country, the sights and sounds of Zenith City were overwhelming. Burgrave continued his rapid pace as he approached the castle.

The castle guards parted to let him through. If they were surprised to see the girls accompanying him, they didn't show it. Burgrave led them into the cool interior of the castle, through a series of winding corridors. The walls were illustrated with a mural that illustrated the founding of Zenith City, but Suzanne, still hurrying to keep up, didn't have time to take it in.

The official slowed down as he approached two

enameled doors. There were no handles or knobs on the doors, not even a keyhole. Both bore the Altairi insignia, but instead of dyed fabric or branded metal, the door was made of a material that glowed and pulsed with energy. Suzanne turned around; Brit and Mikayla were also staring at the twin insignias.

"Isn't that Energite?" Brit whispered.

Suzanne nodded, amazed. Wasn't there an Energite shortage? Things in Zenith City were making less and less sense.

Of course, Burgrave also heard the whisper. "The Royal Seal. It is a necessary precaution. Even in," he paused, searching for the right words, "such times of scarcity."

He placed one hand on each of the insignias. They glowed brightly until they were pure white. When the insignias looked ready to explode, there was a loud click, and the heavy doors scraped open.

As splendid as Zenith City was, nothing could have prepared the girls for the throne room. Magnificent chandeliers hung from the ceiling, scattering soft light everywhere. Tapestries, each bearing the Altairi insignia, covered the walls. Even the floor was a beautiful mosaic of gold and silver.

At the other end of the room was an empty throne.

"Where's the king?" Brit whispered, her words echoing around the chamber.

As if on cue, a hand appeared behind one of the tapestries, pulling it back. An NPC stepped out from behind the tapestry, wearing a flowing crimson robe and a bejeweled crown of Energite. Curly gray hair flanked his pale, narrow face. He straightened his robes and walked across the room to his throne, unfazed by the three strangers before him.

As the tapestry swung back into place, Suzanne caught a glimpse of the door concealed behind it, marked with a green letter *H*. Suzanne did a double take. Was that the door to a hack point? She'd coded two hack points in Io, one each in the capitals of Pyxis and Altair. They were places where she could edit the code from within if she needed to. But NPCs couldn't get into hack points, so what was the king doing in there?

Before she could puzzle it out, the king was speaking. "Greetings, strangers," he said, "I am Ramses, King of Altair."

Burgrave kneeled and bowed until he his head touched the floor. Remembering Burgrave's caution, Suzanne followed his example and bowed low to the king.

"No need for such formalities," he said. "For you three are heroes, if I am not mistaken. Defenders of Oppold, yes?"

"Yeah," Brit replied, standing back up. "Nice to meet you."

Burgrave looked scandalized at her lack of decorum, but the king merely laughed.

"You must be Lady Brit," he chuckled. "I've heard you gave our guards below quite a fright. Something about smashing Burgrave's pumpkin, if I am not mistaken?"

Brit stared fearlessly back at the king.

"King Ramses," Suzanne said, "thank you for agreeing to meet with us. We're strangers from a—"

The king raised his hand to silence her. "I know

who you are," he said curtly. She bridled at an NPC interrupting her, but she wanted to hear what the king had to say.

"I hear that you are powerful fighters. If that is the case, you may be able to help me after all."

"A monster has taken up residence in my kingdom. It has taken over the Decan Caves, far to the north of here, along the border of Pyxis. Because of the monster, we cannot establish a secure border against those savages, but between the war and the need for increased security, I find I am short on men. We have reason to believe the monster is in possession of a massive lode of Energite. Surely you have heard of the shortage?"

The Energite jewels in the king's crown pulsed in the glittering light of the chandeliers.

"Such a lode would do much for addressing our needs."

"What makes you so sure we can handle it?" Mikayla asked.

The king smiled the same thin smile. "It should be nothing for the heroes of Oppold. Naturally, you shall have the full support of the royal armorer, as well as a detachment of soldiers to assist you in battle."

The king walked back to his throne and sat down. "Of course, the mission will not be without danger. The monster has already killed several strong warriors."

"What do you think?" Brit said, turning to Mikayla and Suzanne. "Is this our quest?"

Mikayla whispered to Brit, "We need to know what the monster is before we agree to fight it."

"It is a Lamia," Burgrave said. Suzanne jumped with surprise—she didn't think the official would hear them, but she had forgotten about his heightened senses.

"A what?" Brit said.

"A Lamia," the king replied. "An abomination. Its body is both woman and serpent. Burgrave has more intelligence on the matter."

Burgrave nodded. "Such information is highly classified. Only if you choose to accept can I share the rest with you."

Brit and Mikayla turned towards Suzanne, the same questioning look on both their faces. Suzanne nodded. The name was all she needed to know. The Lamia was designed to be one of the later bosses in the game. It shouldn't have spawned until the girls reached the advanced classes. Maybe the uncannily strong NPCs had triggered its appearance early. Still, at least the monster was something she had designed. Even if their characters were still in initial classes, she felt confident the girls could handle it.

"I appreciate the danger this task would place you in," the king said. "Take the next day to decide. But by sundown tomorrow, I will have your answer."

"We don't need an extra day," Brit said. "Let's go monster hunting!"

Suzanne opened her Quest Log. Sure enough, SLAY THE LAMIA was now at the top of their list.

Chapter 12

"So what's a llama?" Brit asked.

"Lam–EE–a," Suzanne corrected her.

"Whatever. How do we kill it?"

"Same as everything else," Suzanne said. "Hit it until it runs out of health."

After their meeting with the king, Burgrave had shown them out of the castle, promising to find them later with more information. They were wandering Zenith City, taking in the sights of Io's largest metropolis.

Their conversation caught the attention of inquisitive NPCs, but Brit stared them all down. There was something about the Zenith Citizens that became more apparent as the girls spent more time walking the city. In Oppold and on the Grand Highway there was a sense of anxiety, of the Altairi–Pyxian War looming overhead.

But the war seemed to be the last thing on the Zenith Citizens' minds. Walking around the city, the girls heard more arguments over minstrels than foreign policy. NPCs bickered pleasantly over which designers were superior, and how much was an appropriate cost for enameled armor. Nobody seemed to care that the Pyxians had such a strong foothold in Altair, and no one seemed concerned about the proposition of Zenith City being invaded.

No, Suzanne thought, there wasn't much cause for concern in Zenith City. Obviously the raiders would pick off small towns instead of trying to sack the metropolis. Even if some bandits got frisky, they'd have the Royal Guard to contend with—assuming they could even make it up the elevators.

They looked in at every merchant stall and shop, looking for stronger weapons and armor. Every item they saw was designed for decoration, rather than fighting.

"No, no," a merchant assured them. "These are the best spears in all of Zenith City! My grandfather killed a dragon with the one you're holding, miss."

Holding the spearhead between her thumb and index finger, Brit bent it backwards, so that the point was touching the shaft.

"What was the dragon made out of? Pillows?"

Unfortunately, Brit's little display broke the spear into pixels. Even in Io, you break it, you buy it, was the law of the land, and while the spear might not have been useful as a weapon, purchasing it put a serious dent in the girls' supply of gold.

"They're all selling junk," Brit grumbled as they walked away. The only items the girls purchased (besides the broken spear) were three maps. The cartographer was disappointed when they went for the standard parchment models.

Suzanne had to agree with Brit. None of the merchants selling weapons had particularly high smithing skills—all their weapons were similarly fragile. But then where did the Royal Guard get their weapons?

They found out soon enough. Burgrave and a detachment of guards found them in the next square and brought them to the barracks of the City Guard, where they were decked out in new gear.

"Now this," Brit said, modeling her new plate mail in a mirror, "is treatment I could get used to."

Suzanne was as fascinated by the mirror as she was by the armory full of items the NPCs had made. And the NPCs had made these items through the forging process. Suzanne thought about trying to track the weapon-smiths down, but she figured Brit and Mikayla would rather go monster hunting than learn about smithery.

"That Ramses guy is kind of a creep," Mikayla said.

"What makes you say that?" Suzanne asked.

Mikayla shrugged and tried on a different shield. "I don't know. He just seemed like a scumbag. Maybe it was the way he laughed?"

"Whatever," Brit said. "You have to deal with annoying kings in every game."

Suzanne stretched and yawned. She was beginning to get tired. Not her character, but Suzanne herself. She'd have to get some real sleep soon. Maybe tonight they would log out and log some hours in real beds. Suzanne knew the rock-hard NPC beds wouldn't get her the requisite eight hours.

She wondered how long it had been in the real world. There wasn't a one-to-one ratio between Io time and real time: Io time sped up and slowed down depending on what was happening. Suzanne thought she ought to put a real-world clock somewhere in the game, just so she could keep tabs on that.

Satisfied with their armor, the girls tried out new weapons. A bland NPC provided them with practice dummies to try the weapons out on.

Brit immediately gravitated towards a titanic halberd that rivaled the giant Crux's hammer.

"We're going to be traveling," Mikayla said. "You might want something lighter."

"Please, I can lift this thing with one hand," Brit

replied, and she did so, grunting under the weapon's weight.

Suzanne rolled her eyes. She snuck up behind Brit, who was now attempting a bicep curl with the halberd. Suzanne gave her a hard shove in the back, and as before, Brit lost her balance and went tumbling to the ground.

Mikayla burst out laughing and Suzanne joined in. Even Brit laughed, once she got over her indignation.

"You've got to stop falling for that," Suzanne laughed.

Brit chuckled, but then her face lit up. "That gives me an idea," she said, standing up and dusting herself off. She left the titanic halberd where it had fallen, the floor cracked by the impact.

The next halberd she tried out was considerably smaller, with an axe blade on both ends. Brit twirled the new double-ended halberd over her head. The blades whirling, she approached the dummies. Then, like lightning, she struck out with the halberd and neatly sliced one of the dummies in half. Turning with her momentum, Brit swung the other blade of the halberd up, slicing the dummy in half again, this time vertically. Quartered, the dummy fell to pieces on the floor.

"Not bad," Brit said, hefting the halberd with one hand. "This'll do."

While Mikayla tested out her thrusts and slashes with a variety of one and two-handed swords, Suzanne occupied herself with the daggers. She wanted more variety in their sizes, larger ones for melee fighting and smaller ones for throwing. The armory had all that and more: trick daggers that double as grappling hooks, daggers with vials for poison, and daggers so small she could hide them in the palm of her hand.

When she fought, Suzanne never thought about the weight of the weapon in her hand. It became an extension of her character's arm and she wielded it unconsciously. But in the armory she was experiencing the weapons as items. These daggers had a weight to them. She ran her finger along the edge of the blade, but when she wasn't attacking the dagger was dull.

After picking out a healthy selection, she went

to find the smiths working on her armor, and did her best to describe where she wanted to be able to attach sheaths. The smiths smiled, but they'd clearly never heard of someone hiding a dagger in their shoe before.

Fully equipped, the girls were taken to the guest wing of Zenith Castle. Their room was just as fancy as every other part of the castle, with gilded sheets covering their rock-hard mattresses.

"I say we log out," Suzanne said. "Get some real sleep. Log back in tomorrow ready to whup some Lamia tail."

"Sounds good to me," Mikayla said. She sounded as exhausted as Suzanne felt.

"I'd say this was a success for day one of Operation Epic Game," Brit yawned. Lazily, she gestured to open her Menu.

Suzanne mimicked her. She opened her Player Menu and navigated to END SESSION.

"See you in a second," she said, and then she was back in her bedroom, back in reality, just for the night.

Chapter 13

Suzanne's alarm went off at five-thirty. She was out of bed in a flash. When she looked in the bathroom mirror she saw her eyes were red and puffy, but she was fully awake with excitement.

When she came back to the bedroom, Mikayla was deflating the air mattress. They didn't exchange any words, only smiles.

Brit did not share their enthusiasm. She had shared Suzanne's bed last night and was still conked out. When Suzanne tried to shake her awake, Brit threw a pillow at her.

"I don't get up this early for school," she grumbled. "Fuck off."

"Come on!" Suzanne said. "We have to kill the Lamia!" But neither that argument nor any of the others she made could get Brit up. Brit's obstinance called for drastic action.

Suzanne grabbed one end of the sheets and Mikayla grabbed the other. They bundled Brit up, dragging her off the bed to the floor. Brit, half-asleep and fully entangled, was powerless to resist.

In Io, Suzanne realized, they would never be able to push around Brit the Fighter. She was much easier to deal with when she was five feet tall.

Despite her complaining, Brit was the first to slide her TII helmet on. She slumped back into the beanbag. Mikayla was sitting in the desk chair. Suzanne took a last look at their still bodies before joining them in virtual reality.

She sat up in Ramses's castle. Brit and Mikayla had equipped their armor. Suzanne just got hers on when there was a knock on the door.

Burgrave appeared, flanked by two members of the City Guard.

"Good morning," he said, as politely as ever.

"Morning," Suzanne replied, stretching. She felt her mind synchronizing with her player character's body. She was ready for the day.

"It is time we left," Burgrave said blandly. "We have many miles to cover."

The girls followed Burgrave back to the main plaza of Zenith City. They waited a few minutes before the elevator arrived to take them down to the suburbs.

After spending so much time in Zenith City, Suzanne had a hard time adjusting to the shadow of the suburbs. It was bizarre to think that the huge structure towering over them was the base of the metropolis. And while there were plazas and fountains in the suburb, much the same as above, these fountains did not run, and the plazas were empty of the bustle and chatter that gave them life.

Despite the gloomy surroundings, Suzanne was bursting with excitement. In the suburbs they met up with the rest of the soldiers who'd be accompanying them. Looking over the NPCs in their gleaming Altairi armor, Suzanne felt downright unstoppable.

This Lamia was going to be a piece of cake, she thought.

Suzanne, Brit, and Mikayla crammed into a tiny carriage alongside Burgrave. Brit's armor filled nearly half of the carriage by itself. Eventually they stopped so she could step out and unequip her gear so they could all breathe better.

Burgrave turned out to be an awkward traveling companion. He said nothing for the first half-hour of the ride, imposing silence on the girls as well. To pass the time, he produced a whittling knife and a block of wood from his inventory and began to whittle the block into a small horse. But even as he whittled, he still watched the girls.

"May I ask why you are smiling?" Burgrave said.

Suzanne hadn't realized she was.

"I guess I'm just excited," she said. "To, um, fight the Lamia."

He shook his head. "You should never be excited for such a battle. The Lamia is a deadly creature. How little we know about it makes the monster deadlier still. There is an old Altairi saying: The unknown is the greatest enemy."

Suzanne hadn't thought an NPC could make her feel guilty for smiling. But then, Burgrave didn't know this was all just a game.

"Hey, Burgrave," Brit said. "Where we come from we've got a saying: Relax. We'll take care of the monster and get you back to your king in one piece."

The bald NPC didn't respond, but turned to look out the carriage's small window, still whittling away.

The villages they passed were all ghost towns much like the villages they had seen while walking to Zenith City. Suzanne noticed that Burgrave's normally impassive expression had been replaced by a look of deep sadness.

After thirty minutes he turned to address the girls again.

"We'll be stopping in a small village named Reinke. The three of you will be staying in the inn."

"What about the townsfolk?" Suzanne asked.

"The Pyxians butchered them," Burgrave said.

Suzanne thought she heard a note of anger in his voice, but she could not be sure.

"Raiders? They killed everyone?"

"Those who survived are now in Zenith City," he said. "This town is close to the border. Apparently, it was one of the first casualties of the war."

"Apparently?"

"That is what King Ramses's scouts reported," the official replied.

A question had been bothering Suzanne, and she realized that Burgrave would be the NPC to ask.

"What are they like? Pyxians?"

Burgrave looked down at his whittling. "They are like me. Or rather, I am like them."

Suzanne thought that she should have known better than to expect a straight answer from Burgrave, but before she could ask for more explanation, he began to speak again.

"What I mean is that were it not for my parents coming to the kingdom of Altair, I would be on the other side of this war. My father was a Pyxian merchant, my mother his bodyguard. They came to

Altair many years ago, before Ramses consolidated the power of the kingdom into Zenith Castle, long before this conflict began."

"So you're fighting your own people," Brit said. Her words came out incredulous, as a question.

"No," Burgrave replied, still whittling intently. "No, my people are the people of Altair. I have lived in Altair my whole life. I have never been to Pyxis. By blood I may be Pyxian, but where it counts," he said, tapping his forehead to indicate his brain, "I am a Citizen of Altair."

"But how can you fight against your blood?"

Burgrave looked up from his whittling and held out the toy horse so the girls could see. He had shaved it down to just a sliver.

"Why is it that the wood does not pixelate when I shave it lengthwise? Yet when I break it in half . . . " His voice trailed off as he snapped the head of the horse off from its neck. It pixelated and the pixels drifted away, like dandelions in the breeze.

"I don't know," Mikayla said, shooting a nervous glance towards Suzanne. "That's just how it works."

"Or how it was designed. The Pyxians believe the world was designed, and everything in it was designed as well. That includes them, and me, and you."

His words sent a thrill of fear through Suzanne. How could there be a whole country of self-aware programs?

Burgrave, mistaking the expression on her face for confusion, strove to explain himself. "It is a metaphor they use for explaining the inexplicable. They believe that all things happen for a purpose, and all things have a purpose, no matter how difficult that purpose might be to see. And they live their lives in service to that purpose, no matter how grand, no matter how small."

He cleared his throat before continuing. "I was raised with such beliefs. For years I agonized over what my purpose might be, what function I could serve."

He looked towards Mikayla and smiled. "Like Mikayla, I wanted to help as many people as possible.

And so I came to realize that by serving the Kingdom I would fulfill my purpose."

"But how can you be sure that's what you're supposed to do?" Mikayla asked.

"Of course, I cannot," he replied. "But knowing what I know, being who I am, I am confident that this is the best path for me to follow."

He stuck the whittling knife back into his belt. "Nothing is ever certain," he said. "It is wise to embrace what best you know."

Suzanne spent the rest of the ride pondering those words, lost in thought until Burgrave quietly said, "We have arrived."

Glad to be free of the carriage, Suzanne went outside to stretch and relax. Brit and Mikayla followed her out of the carriage. The soldiers busied themselves setting up sentries for the night, which struck Suzanne as odd, until she remembered that the village was abandoned. Did that mean that monsters could attack the village? Come to think of it, Suzanne had no idea what kind of monsters there were around Reinke.

She saw that Brit and Mikayla were off somewhere, so Suzanne figured she might as well check
the rest of the village out. If she ran into any monsters—well, she could use the experience points.

As she walked further into Reinke, Suzanne saw
soldiers breaking down abandoned buildings for
firewood. They waved to her as she came closer, but
they didn't make any effort to start a conversation
with her. She figured that they all had jobs to do,
and besides, most NPCs weren't known for their
conversational skills.

But then she heard a voice. It was gruff and
menacing, and it came from somewhere nearby in
the village. The voice sounded familiar, but Suzanne
couldn't quite place it.

"Weird being back here," the voice said.

Something in the NPC's tone told Suzanne to be
careful. She ducked behind a wall and used Shadow
Walk, one of the Rogue class's special abilities. The
move drained most of her Energite, but she'd have
plenty of time to restore that before she fought the
Lamia.

Suzanne felt a weird tingle originate at the base of her spine and spread across her body. She knew that she wasn't really invisible, but as long as she didn't bump into any NPCs, they wouldn't notice her. Satisfied in her stealth, she headed towards where she had heard the voice.

A large group of soldiers had gathered in the town square. They had taken off their helmets and set their weapons down. Suzanne realized she had never seen members of the Altairi Army relaxing before. Suzanne marveled at how the AI kept running, animating the NPCs even when the girls weren't around.

"I get ya, Corvus," another one of the soldiers said in a high-pitched voice. "Place brings back memories. Why, right over there, I—"

The gruff-voiced soldier growled, "Quiet, idiot. Those girlies are around here somewhere."

Suzanne's breath caught in her throat. Even though he was sitting with his back towards her, facing the other soldiers, Suzanne remembered where she had heard that voice before. The scars on the back of the soldier's head confirmed it: it was the leader of the Mongrels, the Pyxian raiders who had burned down Oppold.

But that didn't make any sense. What would Pyxian raiders be doing in Altair's army?

Before she could move, Corvus spoke again.

"We're to keep a low profile, remember? Our job's not on until after they deal with the Lamia."

The high-pitched soldier laughed. "Yessir. Then is it time for . . . " Instead of finishing the sentence, the soldier mimed gutting someone with a wickedly curved knife.

"Except the big one," Corvus snarled. "She's mine."

Suzanne pulled a throwing knife off of her belt. With the Shadow Walk, she'd be able to get a few attacks in before they'd know it was her. But the other soldiers gathered in the square were listening intently to what Corvus said, like he was leading them, too. Suzanne knew she couldn't take them all on. She had to find the other girls.

As quietly as she could, she backed away from the

square. The timer on the Shadow Walk was running out, so she ducked behind a house before she became fully visible again. Suzanne waited and listened for anyone who might be following her. Convinced she was okay, she started to run, looking for Brit and Mikayla.

Chapter 14

Suzanne kept running until she saw Brit and Mikayla.

"Yo, Suze!" Brit shouted, waving. "Where'd you go? We were off farming some goblins. I leveled up!"

"Corvus is here," Suzanne gasped.

"Who?" Mikayla asked.

"Corvus. The leader of the Mongrels."

Mikayla pulled out her estoc. "Where? We've got to tell the soldiers."

"No," Suzanne said. "He's one of the soldiers. All the Mongrels are."

"What are you talking about?" Brit said.

Suzanne shared the conversation she had overheard.

Mikayla bit her lip. "Could it be anything else? Like what if there were just two NPCs who looked the same?"

Suzanne shook her head. "It could be that the game code cloned a character accidentally. But even if it did, it's statistically impossible for us to have encountered the clone already."

"Unless the code's glitching," Brit said. "Wouldn't be the first time."

Suzanne nodded. "But that's a glitch that doesn't make sense. It's not like features disappearing or an actual clone. This would be the game's AI designing two identical characters, giving them the same memories and triggering their appearance at two completely different towns, weeks apart from each other."

Suzanne fell silent for a second, lost in thoughts. After a moment of intense concentration she said, "Yeah, it just doesn't make sense."

"To be honest," Mikayla said, "none of that made sense to me."

Brit laughed. "I guess if you say it can't happen then we've got to believe you."

"We have to tell Burgrave," Mikayla said.

"Why? He has to be in on it. There's no way he couldn't know," Brit replied.

What if Corvus and the Mongrels had invaded the Altairi Army? The girls could handle them—they'd done it before—and back then none of them was higher than a level three. Now, they had close to a month of in-game experience behind them, and what's more, they had weapons. They could handle the Mongrels.

And if Burgrave was in on it? Well, then they'd have to deal with him, too.

Brit said, as if she had read Suzanne's mind, "Well, at least things are never boring here."

"I don't know," Mikayla said. "I still think we should tell Burgrave."

"No way!" Brit said. "This is a speed run! No time for military investigations in a speed run!"

Mikayla looked like she was about to argue, but something over Brit's shoulder caught her attention. "Someone's coming this way," she said. Then a smile broke out on her face. A minute later, Picciotto arrived at the edge of the village.

"What are you doing here?" Suzanne asked, happy to see a friendly face.

"Conspiring in loud whispers, same as you," came the Troubadour's glib reply.

Suzanne noticed he was wearing armor bearing the Altairi insignia.

"Did you join the army?" she asked.

"Pretty much had to. There wasn't much work around Zenith City. But what about you three? You never mentioned you were heroes."

Suzanne laughed. "That's taking things a bit far."

Picciotto's smile wavered. "You should hear the soldiers talk about you lot. If rumors are to believed, then the three of you don't need any backup. Anyway, there's going to be a meeting in the inn shortly, and his shortness wishes for you to attend."

"We'll be there in a minute," Suzanne said.

"Okay," Picciotto said. "But don't take too long or you'll miss the scintillating conversation."

He walked off humming. Once he was out of earshot, Suzanne turned back to the other girls. "Are we going to talk to Burgrave?"

Brit shook her head. "If he's in on it, our only advantage is that he doesn't know we know."

"But if he isn't?" Suzanne said.

Her question lingered on the walk back to town. The sun was setting, casting fantastic shadows from the tall trees. In the real world, sunset was when the cicadas got loud, when the streetlights lit up and cast the world in shades of nocturnal orange. Evenings in the real world hummed; in Io there was only the cry of distant monsters, of fires crackling in the Altairi Army camp.

As the girls passed through the town, they saw soldiers polishing their armor and weapons. The most restless sparred with wooden swords or did target practice with the signs hanging from buildings. Suzanne wondered if they were staving off boredom or fear of the monster waiting for them in the Decan Caves.

Reinke's inn was much larger than the one in Oppold. Pushing through the double doors, Suzanne saw that it had been emptied of tables. At one end of the inn a fire blazed. Rows of chairs filled the room, occupied by the soldiers. Those that couldn't find seats stood in the back of the room.

All the soldiers faced the fire where Burgrave sat. On his right side were three soldiers, two Paladins and a Berserker. To his left were three empty chairs. Seeing the girls enter, he motioned for them to join him. Squeezing past the soldiers, they made they way to the front of the room, doing their best not to step on anyone's toes.

Most of the soldiers were without their armor. Suzanne saw how young they looked and how uncertain. With their helmets on, they seemed like a much more daunting force. Helmetless, she could see that they were young men, and that some of them were afraid.

Last to come in was a group of soldiers still in full

regalia. Suzanne nudged Mikayla. Those were the Mongrels. They leaned up against the wall. While the other soldiers chatted nervously, the armored latecomers remained silent, their faces obscured by helmets.

Satisfied the company was all present, Burgrave rose and said, "Tomorrow we face the Lamia. The monster has plagued our land for long enough. No more."

Two soldiers stood and set up a map of the Decan Caves and the surrounding area. "This is the layout of the caves as best we know. The entrance is located here," Burgrave said, pointing with his sword. "Wollman's squadron will scout ahead and attempt to verify the monster's location within the caves."

One of the Paladins, a well-trimmed beard covering his face, stood and walked over to the map. "My men and I will try to locate the beast. We'll also be leaving torches so the rest of you won't have to stumble in the dark."

Burgrave spoke directly to Wollman. "Travel as

lightly as you can. You are not to engage the monster, only to discover its location. Once that is confirmed, the second team will move in."

The red-haired Berserker stood. "That's me, right?" He spoke up. "You lot in the back are with me. We're to do first incursion, figure out its health bar and the like. Heavy armor boys."

Brit nudged Suzanne. The Mongrels seemed unfazed by being thrown first into the flame. But then, they had talked a big game in Oppold and that hadn't exactly gone the way they planned. Suzanne was glad she knew what the Lamia was capable of. Otherwise, they'd be relying on their enemies to tell them the monster's weaknesses.

"Thank you, Eirik," Burgrave said. "Your position is most fraught, as it will be before we are fully aware of the Lamia's capabilities. Once those are determined, fall back for the third team."

"Assuming we don't finish it ourselves," Eirik retorted.

Burgrave smiled thinly but did not reply. He turned to the girls. "Brit, Mikayla, and Suzanne will lead the third team in once we have ascertained the monster's skill set. You three will be accompanied by Picciotto and his men."

Picciotto winked, but stayed seated. Samara was leaning forward, staring intently at the map, her chin resting on her hands. It was good to know they would be going into caves with NPCs they trusted.

"Oh great," Brit muttered, "we're going in with our own marching band."

Suzanne had to cough to cover her laughter.

Burgrave continued outlining the plan. There were two more teams: a relief squad headed by the other Paladin, named Engel, and the command team that Burgrave would personally oversee. Then, just to make sure everyone understood his or her role, Burgrave went over the entire plan again.

Concluding, he said, "I need not remind you that we are working from imperfect information. As always, it is best to rely first on yourself and second on those fighting beside you. Only then should you trust in what you have heard. Our greatest advantage in this battle is that we are not monsters. We are Citizens of Altair, and as such, victory is our lifeblood."

With that, Burgrave dismissed the meeting. The soldiers filed out of the inn, into the night, taking their expectations and apprehensions for the next day with them.

Chapter 15

They set out early the next morning. They marched north without speaking, only the trudging of boots and scraping of armor breaking the silence.

Suzanne marched near the rear of the column, alongside Brit and Mikayla. The girls had as little to say as the soldiers. All minds, artificially intelligent or naturally, were focused on the task at hand and the Lamia that lay waiting for them.

All minds except for Picciotto the Troubadour's. While his two companions marched silently, the Troubadour hummed ceaselessly. With his long eyelids drooping, he looked half asleep. Suzanne marveled that he was able to find his way safely over the uneven ground. Without knowing, she found herself grateful the Troubadour was marching beside them, grateful for his soft humming breaking the monotony.

Brit was less enthusiastic about the musician.

"I wish he'd hum something else," she muttered.

Mikayla nodded. "You'd think a Troubadour would know more than one song."

Suzanne chuckled. Annoyed, Brit turned towards her.

"What? Don't tell me you're enjoying this."

Before Suzanne could answer, Picciotto was making his way over to the girls.

"I think he heard you," Mikayla said.

"Sorry if it bothers you," the Troubadour said, in a voice as musical as his hum. "It's the only marching tune I know."

"Well, why don't you just make a new one up?" Brit asked.

Suzanne realized that she had never explained Troubadours to the girls, and so they didn't know what the class's special ability was. When they were picking their classes, they all chose ones that could fight up close. But Troubadours were a support class, weak on their own but excellent on teams.

"You three aren't from Altair, right? Do they have Troubadours where you come from?"

"Yeah," Mikayla said. "But we don't send them to war."

"Ah," the Troubadour said. "So you have musicians. Not Troubadours."

"And the difference is?" Brit asked.

Suzanne could tell her patience was wearing thin, and that Picciotto was as laconic with his answers as he was with everything else. Answering for him, she said, "Troubadours work best when supporting others. When they make music, it powers up their allies."

Picciotto nodded. "So when I hum, we march faster. And when I don't . . . "

He gestured to the marching soldiers, who were showing the first signs of fatigue. Suzanne realized they had been marching uphill for the past hour, but she hadn't noticed the change in terrain. There was a lot to be said for Troubadours. Having Picciotto on their side would make the battle with the Lamia significantly easier.

Satisfied that he had explained himself, the Troubadour began humming again. Immediately the other soldiers perked up and began marching faster, as if they'd just gotten their second wind.

Slowly the mountain containing the Decan Caves came into focus. When it grew so large on the horizon as to dominate the skyline, the company broke to rest. The sun was still rising, but at these altitudes the air was cool. Suzanne took advantage of the break to catch up with Picciotto.

Most of the soldiers paced, too nervous to relax. Those that did still wore the worried look they'd left town with that morning. Compared to the rest of the troops, Picciotto and his gang looked like they were on holiday.

The Troubadour was sitting in the shade of a tree, whistling a light tune to himself and his companions. Samara was restringing her bow and the massive Desmond was lying on the grass, one of his shields serving as a makeshift pillow. As Suzanne approached, Picciotto whistled a new tune. Suzanne was impressed by his ability, until she remembered he was an NPC and that the game was making the sounds for him. Still, it beat the nervous chatter of the rest of the company.

"What's this tune do?" she asked.

Picciotto finished the bar he was whistling before answering.

"Absolutely nothing. Just something to pass the time."

He broke into a goofy grin. Suzanne understood why she'd felt such a natural liking for the Troubadour. He almost seemed like a real person. The only thing he seemed to have in common with the other soldiers was the gray icon over his head.

"May I ask you a question?" she asked.

"You just did," he replied.

Samara leaned over and smacked him in the head. "Be helpful, or she'll gut you," the Sniper teased.

Suzanne couldn't help laughing at their antics.

"Aren't you nervous at all?"

"I'm glad we're here," Samara said. "Beats fighting on the front."

Picciotto nodded. "At least here we get to be the good guys."

"But don't you think Altair is right to defend itself?"

"If you call that defending yourself," Desmond rumbled.

Suzanne was so surprised to hear him speak that it took her a second to register what he had said.

Samara chuckled. "I don't know what you heard in Zenith City," she said, "but there are no heroes in war. Everyone just wants to stay alive and everyone's afraid they'll die. And they're right. Equally scared people, who want to live just as bad, are coming to kill them."

Suzanne wanted to argue that things weren't that simple, at least in Io. But she didn't know how to make her point without telling Picciotto, Samara, and Desmond that they were all NPCs.

"Try not to think so hard," Picciotto said. "You'll do better in the army. Anyway, here come your pals."

Suzanne turned and saw Brit and Mikayla walking over to them.

"Burgrave said it's time to head out," Brit said.

Picciotto sighed heavily, which set Suzanne and Mikayla giggling.

"Come on you big baby," Samara said. "Don't make Desmond carry you."

"He did that one time, and you've never let me live it down," Picciotto indignantly protested.

Winking at the girls, the Sniper whispered, "Just wait till we head back. I bet he fakes an injured foot and Desmond ends up carrying him all the way back to Zenith City."

The soldiers had marched all day to reach the Decan Caves. Now they milled about by the entrance, nerves on a knife's edge as they waited for word from Wollman and his scouting party. They'd gone into the caves thirty minutes before, walking thirty paces before the inky darkness swallowed them.

Burgrave sat cross-legged on the ground in front of the cave entrance, staring into the depths. But no soldiers came out. Wind blew out of the cave with a moaning sound and Suzanne shuddered.

When she was designing the Lamia and its lair,

Suzanne wanted to make it hard for large parties to take the monster on. Now she was regretting that decision. It would be a lot less scary if the whole company could march in and take on the monster at once, but the caves were narrow and dark. If a large party got surprised, they'd get stuck in the retreat. The caves were more like a warren, a maze of interconnecting tunnels. They'd be at the mercy of the Lamia, which, like a snake, saw more with its senses of taste and smell than with its eyes.

Thirty minutes passed, then an hour, then two. The sun was directly overhead, baking the soldiers in the heat. Brit sighed. "Are we just going to stand here all day?"

Suzanne shared her frustration. She wondered what would happen if the girls just went in without waiting for Burgrave's say-so, when a better idea hit her.

She pulled Brit and Mikayla away from the other soldiers. In a whisper, she said, "Let's just log out."

"What?" Mikayla said. "But we'll lose the whole day's progress."

"I'll just reprogram the game to skip this bit,"

Suzanne said. "We'll log back in and go fight the Lamia right away. No waiting around or anything."

"Won't they notice when we just disappear?" Brit asked.

"Who cares?" Suzanne said. "I'll go off old save data so the game won't remember this ever happening."

Brit and Mikayla exchanged a look. "Okay," Mikayla whispered. "I say we do it."

Suzanne opened her Player Menu and navigated to END SESSION. She tapped the blue box that said END SESSION. Nothing happened.

Confused, Suzanne worked her way back through the Menu and selected END SESSION again. And again, nothing happened. There was a dull clunking sound and her Menu closed.

Suzanne looked up, confused. With increasingly frantic gestures, Mikayla was trying again and again to log out. After five tries, she stopped and stared at Suzanne.

"What's going on?"

"I don't know," Suzanne replied. She wasn't whispering anymore.

Brit began trying to log out, but she met with the same dull clunking sound. Suzanne knew what that sound meant. It signaled an illegal game action, like when a player tried to equip a weapon their class couldn't use.

But that couldn't be right. Brit gave up after her first try at logging out. She and Mikayla watched as Suzanne repeated the log-out sequence. After a few more tries the traditional way, Suzanne tried the work around, attempting to restore a previously saved file.

That didn't work either. Confused, Suzanne closed her Menu and sat down on the ground.

"Don't tell me we're stuck here." Brit said it like she was joking, but to Suzanne she looked worried.

"Just give me a second," Suzanne said, but she could hear how shaky her own voice sounded. She had tried logging out, and that didn't work. No other ideas were coming to her.

"What are you waiting for?" Brit demanded. "Get us out of here!"

There was full-on panic in her voice now. That certainly didn't help.

"I'm trying!" Suzanne shouted. "Just shut the fuck up and give me a second to think!"

"Who's the genius who got us trapped here in the first place?" Brit roared.

"Is everything okay?" Burgrave was walking down the slope towards the girls.

"Of course not!" Brit said. Before she could say anything else, Mikayla pushed her out of the way.

"Give us a minute," she said. Burgrave frowned but didn't pursue the matter. Once he was gone, Mikayla wheeled around towards Brit and Suzanne.

"Stop it," she hissed. "Stop fighting. It isn't helping anything. And keep your voices down!"

"Then what do you suggest we do?" Brit asked. She sounded half serious, as if she hoped Mikayla knew the answer.

"What if we kill each other?"

Suzanne immediately understood what Mikayla was saying. Normally, when one of them died, the TII logged them out automatically. They'd lose all their progress, but that was the last thing on Suzanne's mind.

"It might work," she said.

Brit raised her halberd expectantly.

"Wait," Suzanne said, her forehead scrunched up in concentration. If the problem was with the Menu, then dying would log them out, like normal. But if there was a problem with the log-out function itself, then what would happen if they died?

Suzanne explained her fears to Brit and Mikayla. Brit shrugged.

"What's the worst that could happen? We just reload from the last save point, no biggie."

"No, we won't," Suzanne said. "I put permanent death in. So once we die, that's it. We're done if we can't log out."

"So we just start a new game," Brit said.

Suzanne shook her head. "You can't start a new game while anyone else is playing."

"Well we've got to do something," Brit said. "We can't just sit here waiting for your dad to come back."

Mikayla shrugged. "That's not a bad idea. Just find a town somewhere and hole up for the weekend?"

"But that would be months in game time," Suzanne

said. "And I don't know what would happen if we spent that long hooked up to the TII."

"Well, what other choice do we have?" Mikayla asked. "It's not like we can fix the game from inside of it."

Suzanne jumped up in excitement. "You're a genius!" she said. "That's exactly what we have to do! We just need to get to Zenith Castle so I can use the hack point!"

"The what?" Brit said. Suzanne explained the hack point she had seen in Zenith Castle, hidden behind a tapestry in Ramses's throne room.

"If we can get into that room then I can get us out."

"Are you sure?" Mikayla asked.

Suzanne was about to say yes, but she caught herself. Neither Brit nor Mikayla seemed particularly confident in the hack point. At first this annoyed Suzanne, but she could understand their skepticism. After all, before their first session in Io she had assured them that the TII was perfectly safe. And it might still be, a voice within her argued. This could all just be a problem with the Menu. "I don't know if I can fix it.

But once we get to a hack point, at least we'll know what's wrong."

"Okay," said Brit, speaking slowly. "So we go kill this Lamia, and Ramses lets us use his magic room. Then we can log out?"

"Definitely," Suzanne said. Maybe, she thought.

"Sounds good. If that bit of code happens to be working," Brit said. She didn't mean for it to come out as an insult but it still hurt to hear how skeptical Brit was.

"I guess that's the move then," Mikayla said. "Go kill a monster so we can go home. Until then we're stuck sleeping on these bricks."

She didn't seem too excited by the prospect.

"Come on," Suzanne said. "It'll be fun. It's like we're actually going on a quest, you know?"

Brit rolled her eyes. "The Legend of the Trapped Nerds."

Mikayla let out a chuckle. "The Quest for the Magical Hack Point."

"Adventures in Cyberspace?" Suzanne offered.

Brit groaned. "How about you worry about finding the hack point and leave the jokes to us?"

Mikayla was laughing fully now, and Suzanne joined in. It felt good to laugh. She felt the tight feeling in her chest releasing. She took a deep breath. In the real world, her body was motionless on her bed, but here in Io she could fill her lungs with digital air. She could breathe.

And then there was a scream.

Wollman came running out of the cave, screaming. The Paladin was missing his shield and sword and it looked like something had ripped the armor of his arms and chest.

The NPCs closest to the mouth of the caves moved back, away from the flailing Paladin. Desmond the Guardian stepped forward to restrain Wollman.

"Wollman," Burgrave began, but the rest of his words were drowned out by the Paladin's screams.

"Get it off me," he shouted. "Get the coils off me!"

Speaking forcefully, Burgrave said, "Tell me what you saw."

"Too many! Too many, too many, too many!"

"Too many what?" Burgrave said. His eyes were blazing with an intensity Suzanne had never seen before.

But Wollman couldn't answer the question. Whatever he had seen was too horrible. He clamped his eyes shut and began thrashing again, his limbs wild with fear.

"Set him down," Burgrave ordered.

The Guardian released Wollman. Before he could bolt again, Burgrave drew his sword and delivered a staggering blow with the flat of his blade. Dazed, Wollman fell to the ground.

Burgrave turned to face the company of soldiers. "The plan has changed. Eirik, take your men into the cave. Ladies, follow him in. It appears that we underestimated the monster."

Eirik nodded and waved over his men.

"We're going to march around in a dark cave with the Mongrels and snake monsters?" Brit whispered. "Fat chance."

"We can't back out," Suzanne replied. "This is our only way into the hack point."

"Let's just make a break for the castle. We'll take Ramses out and be back in Baltimore before they know what's up."

Mikayla laughed a little too loudly. Her face was peaked and her hands were shaking.

"It's going to be okay," Suzanne whispered. Mikayla nodded but hardly looked reassured.

Eirik sauntered over to the girls. "We'll take point," he said. "No need for caution now, so I'll light the way."

The Berserker drew his sword and unslung his heavy shield from his back. He scraped the blade down the front of the shield, sending up sparks. But Eirik's sword was no ordinary blade; one of the sparks caught on it and the whole weapon burst into flame.

"It's a neat trick," he said. "Doesn't do much but scare in a fight, but pretty good for dark spots."

Still wearing their helmets to hide their faces, Corvus and the Mongrels fell into formation behind Eirik and marched into the cave. The party followed the blazing sword into the darkness.

Chapter 16

The cave was full of noises. Wind moaned out from the depths and the sound of dripping water echoed off the walls until it sounded like a rainstorm. The ground was damp and squished and squelched beneath their greaves. At every sound, Mikayla started a little, as if each would reveal the monster they had come to kill. Every so often the company halted so Eirik could reignite his sword.

Eventually the tunnel narrowed so they had to proceed single file. Eirik, Brit, and Desmond had to stoop to keep going.

"Look," Mikayla said, pointing at the ceiling. The roof of the cave was smooth, free of the stalactites that had covered it earlier. In fact, the tunnel had become perfectly smooth.

"It made this," Samara muttered. "Burrowed straight through the stone."

A thrill of fear spread through Suzanne. The Lamia shouldn't have been able to do something like that. She'd never given it that kind of attack. But the Lamia had clearly modified its home. She couldn't tell Brit or Mikayla—they were probably still freaking over the log-out issues.

"We press on," Eirik said. To Suzanne, it almost sounded like a question.

No one said anything else until they came to a fork in the tunnel. Eirik took a few steps down each route, but they were identical. Shaking his head, the Berserker walked back to the group.

"No way to know."

"What do we do?" one of the Mongrels asked.

For a minute no one spoke, but then Brit said, "Split up. You go left, we go right."

"But how will you see?" Eirik asked.

"I think I've got the answer to that," Samara

said. She pulled an arrow from her quiver. "Blazing Arrow!" she shouted, and the tip of the arrow burst into flames.

"We can light another one if this one starts to go out," she explained.

The flickering light cast long shadows onto Eirik's face. He didn't look pleased at the idea of splitting up.

"Burgrave sent us in together. He meant for us to stay together."

Suzanne, in a quavering voice, said, "We've got to split up and find a larger chamber to fight it in. We're screwed if it attacks us in a tunnel."

Eirik looked uncertain, but he had no alternative.

"Stay safe. And if you find our comrades . . . "

"We'll do our best to get them out," Suzanne said.

Eirik nodded. He led the Mongrels down the left fork. The last thing Suzanne saw, before the darkness swallowed them, was the Berserker's red hair.

When their footsteps were an echo along the wall, Picciotto spoke up.

"Shall we?" he asked. There was no flippancy in his tone.

"Let's," Brit said. Samara passed her the torch. Holding it in front of her, Brit led the way further into the Lamia's lair.

The tunnel wound its way through the darkness. Suzanne was grateful that at least there were no more forks. If they never found their way out of the tunnels then they'd be trapped in the Decan Caves forever. Trapped in the game . . . Suzanne shook her head, trying to dispel those thoughts. One thing at a time. First the Lamia, then the hack point.

After stumbling through the semidarkness for a while, the tunnel widened, enough so Brit and Desmond could stand upright and the party could move forward without having to walk single file. They had to stop so Samara could ignite a second arrow. Suzanne wondered how much Energite she had left—the Blazing Arrows were a special attack, and every new one drained Samara's reserve. They needed to find the Lamia soon or they'd be fighting it in the dark.

"Wait," Mikayla said. "I hear something."

"Wasn't me," replied Picciotto. Nobody laughed.

"Up ahead," Mikayla said. Then her eyes widened. "It's coming this way!"

Before Suzanne could ask what was coming their way, the tunnel filled with a whispering sound, like two sheets of paper rubbing against each other. Following the sound, they came into a wider chamber, crisscrossed with tunnels. Lying in the middle of the room was an item. Brit went over and added it to her inventory.

"It's Eirik's sword," she said.

"He wouldn't have dropped it," Mikayla said.

But then where was Eirik? And for that matter, where were the Mongrels? The way forward was obvious—the noise was coming clearly from one of the tunnels. But where would it lead?

"Desmond, take the front," Samara said.

Holding a shield with each hand, the Guardian advanced to the front of their party. The whispering sound grew louder, echoing off the cave walls, until it seemed to come from all sides. They moved forward slowly—too slowly, Suzanne thought. The arrow would burn out soon.

But before it did, they found the source of the noise. The tunnel opened up again into a huge cavern. The roof was so high that the light from the torch didn't reach the top. But the girls hardly noticed, because they were staring at the floor and walls. Covering every inch of the floor, coiled around rocks and dangling from stalactites, the girls saw what had been making the commotion: snakes.

Mikayla covered her mouth with her hands and backed away.

Suzanne tried to make out where the path continued, but her eyes were distracted by the shifting patterns of snakes. Their patterns were mesmerizing. Then she saw an anaconda, as long as a bus, launch itself at her.

Reflexively she drew her dagger. Ducking under the snake's mouth, she sliced its underside open. The snake fell on top of her. She almost collapsed under its weight, but managed to heave it off. Then she jumped back; hundreds of tiny snakes wriggled free of the large one, squirming over to the mass of snakes.

"It hurtssssss usssssss," a voice hissed. Picciotto stopped playing.

Suzanne and the others looked around, but they couldn't see who had spoken. From wall to wall there was nothing but snakes. But now they were neither ignoring nor advancing on the party. They were bunching together on the opposite side of the cavern, their bodies wriggling over each other with such speed that Suzanne couldn't tell where one serpent ended and the next began.

"We hurt it," the voice hissed.

"Who said that?" Brit demanded. "Where are you?"

Then they heard a sound like a whispered chuckle. A horrible thought occurred to Suzanne. Was this what it sounded like when snakes laughed?

Meanwhile the mass of snakes was rising off the floor. In the fading torchlight, Suzanne saw the mass was taking on the shape of a larger snake. As more snakes joined the mass, it grew larger. Suzanne couldn't tell how big it was as it coiled over itself. Soon it filled a third of the cavern.

Then it began to take on a shape. The snakes fused together, forming a single massive serpent. But then a torso sprouted where the composite snake's head should have been, and arms sprang from the torso. A head grew out of the torso, almost human, but it seemed totally alien to emotions like compassion or love.

The face had no nose. Two slits flared over its mouth, which opened wide into a hideous smile to reveal scythe-like fangs. The bright green eyes had diamond-shaped pupils and no lids.

"I wasssss sssssso hungry," the horrible face said. "Sssssso lonely."

Mikayla let out a frightened squeak and began to back up down the tunnel.

"No," the monster hissed. "Sssstay!"

It lashed its tail right at Mikayla. Desmond shoved her aside and lifted both his shields. The Lamia flicked him aside like he was made of straw.

Desmond slammed into the wall of the cave and fell dazed to the ground.

"Ssssso brave," the monster hissed. "Ssssso ssssstupid."

"Start playing, Pic!" Samara shouted. She loosed an arrow, igniting it as it flew. The fire arrow struck the Lamia in the shoulder, which hissed in rage and ripped the shaft out with its teeth.

Picciotto started playing again, frantically plucking out a tune. Suzanne could barely hear him over the rustling of the Lamia. It slammed its tail at the party again, but this time, they were ready.

Brit ducked under the monster and slammed her halberd down like she was chopping wood. The Lamia roared with pain as the halberd sliced clean through. But in a flash it was speeding across the cavern, its jaw opened wide. It bit down on Brit's armor. Suzanne saw the massive plate mail buckle under the pressure of the Lamia's jaws. Brit's halberd fell from her hand as the torch light flickered out.

"Get off me!" Brit roared through the darkness. She was punching the monster as hard as she could, but she couldn't get leverage while she was dangling in the air, and the Lamia didn't let go.

Samara fired another arrow at the monster, aiming at its neck so as not to hit Brit. Suzanne heard the arrow clatter off the wall, signifying a miss.

"Mikayla," she called into the darkness. "We need you. You can see!"

Suzanne heard a stifled sob and footsteps. It sounded like Mikayla was going to take the monster on. She needed to get another light going, and fast. She groped blindly through her inventory, trying to find something she could light for another torch. She felt a small, smooth stone.

Selecting the item, she saw it pulsed and glowed with Energite. It was an Energite crystal, a random loot drop from a monster. Suzanne squeezed the stone hard, feeling the Energite flow into her as the crystal crumbled to nothing.

Suzanne built all of the game herself. Sure, she'd used map tools she'd found online and had turned to books on mythology for the name generator. But every weapon, every class, and every special attack had been her decision. She could navigate the menus with her eyes shut.

So she knew how to prime a special attack in the darkness, and she knew that the fifth option down for a Rogue was a Naphtha Bomb.

The cavern erupted into light as a ball of fire appeared in her right hand. Suzanne saw Mikayla hacking wildly at the Lamia's underbelly and the snake monster's tail closing around her. Brit still struggled to free herself from the monster's jaws.

"Hey," Suzanne shouted, "over here!"

The Lamia's head swiveled towards her. It dropped Brit and sped towards Suzanne, mouth wide to swallow her whole.

Maybe it was Picciotto's music powering her up, or maybe it was adrenaline. But whatever it was, the fireball in Suzanne's hand swelled until it engulfed her fist. She charged at the Lamia.

Right before the monster reached her, it reared up in pain. Mikayla had stabbed her sword between the scales on its back. With its mouth wide in agony, Suzanne saw her opening. She threw herself into the air and launched the fireball into the monster's mouth.

At first there was darkness as the monster swallowed the flame. Then it began to glow, light bursting through its skin. The Lamia twitched and screamed as it was immolated on Naphtha flames, burned alive from the inside out.

In another moment it was done. With a final, horrible hissing sigh, the Lamia fell to the ground. The corpse burned through and lit the cavern.

Suzanne saw the loot for the battle and automatically added it to her inventory without checking to see what it was. The item vanished into her possession.

The flames cast long shadows on the wall. Brit stood, wincing as she tried to move her bitten shoulder. The shadows and pain made her look old beyond her years.

"Well, fuck," Brit said. "Why didn't you do that sooner?"

Chapter 17

Slowly, Suzanne got to her feet. The body of the Lamia continued to burn, illuminating the cavern. Suzanne saw beyond its burning form another tunnel leading off into the darkness of the cave. She calmed her breathing. Now all they had to do was get back to Zenith City and they could get out of the game.

Brit removed her mangled armor and rotated her arm, trying to work the soreness out. Samara was busy making torches from spare bowstring and arrows. Mikayla was assisting Picciotto in helping Desmond to his feet. The Guardian looked terrible; the Lamia's attacks had rent long gouges in his armor. His breath was ragged and his face was pale. With great effort, they got him standing, but he had to lean on Picciotto with his right arm for support. Suzanne noticed that Desmond's left arm dangled at his side, so wounded as to be useless.

"Well, well, well," Picciotto said. "Who's carrying who?"

Despite the obvious pain he was in, Desmond's face remained calm.

"It's weird being here," Brit said.

Suzanne didn't know if Brit meant in the Decan Caves or in the game, but Suzanne knew she wanted to leave both as soon as possible.

"We can't go back the way we came," Mikayla said. She was peering down the tunnel.

"Why not?" Picciotto asked.

"Desmond can't make it on his own, and the tunnel's too narrow for you to support him."

The Guardian grunted to indicate that he agreed.

"You big lug," Samara said, but her voice was full of tenderness and concern.

"The other path looks wider," Mikayla said. "Let's head that way."

They moved on, much slower than before, hampered by their injuries. Mikayla took the lead, with Samara and Suzanne behind her. Brit and Desmond leaned on each other and Picciotto brought up the rear. It was hard going, especially because the tunnel inclined. But at least the incline suggested they were going up—back to the surface.

Mikayla noticed too. "I can hear rain!"

"Finally, some good news," Picciotto called from the rear.

After another fifteen minutes of walking, Suzanne could hear the sound of rain falling on the hillside. Finally, the tunnel widened into a cave. Stepping around stalagmites, Mikayla led the way out into the downpour. Through the rain Suzanne could see that they were exiting the caves much higher up than they had entered, which made sense, considering how long they'd been walking uphill.

Suzanne couldn't help herself. She let out a joyous yell once they had all stepped out into the rain. The water falling on her face was as refreshing as anything she had ever felt. Only when Desmond complained about drowning in his armor, and the sky lit up with a flash of lightning, did they begin to make their way down the hillside.

They were nearly at the bottom when Picciotto let out a cry of pain. Suzanne whirled around just in time to see the Troubadour stagger and fall, a scythe blade protruding from his back. The scythe was attached to a long chain, the other end of which was held by a soldier wearing the gleaming insignia of the Altairi Army.

"I told you," roared Corvus's voice over the thunder. "I told you I'd be back for you."

Before Suzanne could think she was already charging back up the mountain, dagger in her hand. But she could hardly see in the rain, and the water coursing down the hillside made her ascent impossible.

She heard the twang of bowstrings. From somewhere to her left, Mikayla shouted, "Get down!" and Suzanne threw herself forward as arrows whizzed past overhead. Looking downhill, she only saw sheets of rain. Where were Brit and the rest of the party?

But Suzanne couldn't worry about that. She barely had time to get her footing before the first of the Mongrels was upon her, stabbing at her head with a pike. Suzanne parried the stab and threw a dagger right at the Mongrel's throat—sputtering, he dropped the spear and clutched his throat.

The Mongrel fell to ground. He groaned once and then his body began to distort. He was dying, she realized. With a gasp, the NPC exploded into a cloud of pixels.

He was dead. And Suzanne had killed him.

A wave of nausea swept Suzanne at the sight— they'd never fought human NPCs before, not like this. She saw Mikayla dueling with three Mongrel swordsmen at once. Where had all these other Mongrels come from?

The scythe blade arced high above the battle, heading straight for Mikayla. "Look out!" Suzanne shouted, but before the scythe got close, one of Samara's arrows had knocked it out of the sky.

Mikayla didn't have time to say thanks—she was still fighting three on one. Suzanne watched her friend dance away from a slashing lunge and smash her shield into the Mongrel's face. Another one of the swordsmen tried to get Mikayla from behind, but without looking, she thrust her sword backwards, stabbing the Mongrel in the stomach. He groaned and collapsed.

But Mikayla's maneuver had left her defenseless, and the third Mongrel took the opportunity to slash at her back two-handed.

Lightning struck the top of the hill, illuminating everything in its violent glow. Suzanne saw Mikayla's eyes fill with pain and surprise as she dropped her sword and fell.

In a flash Suzanne was on the Mongrel, her dagger finding a gap in his armor between his helmet and his breastplate. Suzanne felt a frantic pulsing through the handle of the dagger and pushed the blade in further.

The pulsing stopped. Suzanne let go of the handle.

But then a blunt object smashed into the back of her head. She staggered forward and saw her health bar fall away. Then all she could see was the leering face of Corvus.

"I told you," he repeated, his voice as horrible as his psychotic grin. "I told you."

He lifted his axe high. Suzanne felt the strength go from her legs and she sank to her knees. It was all wrong, she thought. They just needed to get back to Zenith City. They just needed to get home.

Corvus didn't bring the axe down. He dropped it. Suzanne saw the Berserker's hands fall to his side, twitching. Looking up she saw his face turning red, his mouth sputtering for breath. His feet, she realized, were dangling inches off the ground, his toes kicking pebbles.

And then she saw what was holding him up.

Brit, her face a mask of anger, held the Mongrel leader by the throat. Corvus gasped for air and kicked at Brit with all his might, but Brit shook him like a rag doll. Only when his feet stopped scrambling did Brit release her vice grip. Corvus fell to the ground, an ugly grimace stamped on his face.

As his pixels spread through the air, Suzanne

realized that Brit was quietly sobbing. Every inch of their bodies was drenched with rain, but the last thing Suzanne saw before she passed out was Brit's face, glistening with tears.

✳

The first thing Suzanne did when she came to was try to log out. When she selected END SESSION, she got the same dull clunk as earlier.

"We tried that," Brit said. "It still isn't working."

Suzanne looked around. She was in a carriage, with Brit and Mikayla. Both of them were watching her with concern in their eyes.

"What happened?" Suzanne asked. Her words came out in a croak.

Mikayla and Brit exchanged looks. "How do you feel?" Mikayla asked. "Are you okay?"

It was only then that Suzanne noticed that both Mikayla and Brit were chained to the walls of the carriage. Suzanne realized her feet were chained to the carriage as well.

"I'm fine," Suzanne croaked. Talking was painful, but everything was painful. That was all wrong. Her health bar was totally full. She shouldn't be feeling pain like this.

"Where's Corvus?"

Mikayla took a deep breath.

"Brit got him."

Suzanne looked at Brit, who didn't look proud. She looked as sick as Suzanne felt.

Fighting past a cloud of pain, Suzanne asked, "Where are we?"

"In a prison transport, on our way to Zenith City."

"A prison transport?" Suzanne wasn't sure she'd heard Mikayla correctly.

"A prison transport," Brit said, flatly. "We've been arrested for murdering an officer in the Altairi Army."

"What? Why?"

"Corvus was a lieutenant," Mikayla explained. "After you passed out, Burgrave and the rest of the army showed up. They saw what happened and took us into custody."

"But he attacked us!" Suzanne said, leaning forward. Her cuffs bit into her arms, so she fell back into a sulk against the carriage wall.

Brit rolled her eyes and snorted with disgust.

"That's not all. We're accused of killing Eirik, too."

"What?"

"Remember how we found his sword? If the Mongrels were good guys, and we're already bad guys, then the fact that I had Eirik's sword is proof enough for these assholes that we killed Eirik."

"That's ridiculous!" Suzanne said. "Look, once we killed the Lamia we were supposed to be heroes! They aren't supposed to arrest us!"

"Yeah, no shit," Brit said.

They spent most of the ride in a pained silence. Suzanne tried to gather her thoughts, but the pain made it hard for her to concentrate. When her brain finally began to clear up, she noticed the road had become smoother and realized they must have caught back up with the Grand Highway. They'd be in Zenith City in a matter of hours, right by the hack point.

"Listen," she said, leaning forward against her restraints. "We're going to escape. We've got to escape."

"How?" Brit demanded. "In case you haven't noticed, we're chained up in here and there's a whole kingdom against us."

"It doesn't matter," Suzanne said. "We've got to."

"I agree," Mikayla said, "but what's your plan?"

The other girls stared at Suzanne expectantly. She cleared her throat.

"I might have an idea."